Sparrow, Always

Also by Gail Donovan

Sparrow Being Sparrow
Sparrow Spreads Her Wings

Sparrow, Always

Gail Donovan

Illustrated by
Elysia Case

A
atheneum
ATHENEUM BOOKS
FOR YOUNG READERS
New York Amsterdam/Antwerp London
Toronto Sydney/Melbourne New Delhi

atheneum

ATHENEUM BOOKS FOR YOUNG READERS
An imprint of Simon & Schuster Children's Publishing Division
1230 Avenue of the Americas, New York, New York 10020
For more than 100 years, Simon & Schuster has championed authors and the stories they create. By respecting the copyright of an author's intellectual property, you enable Simon & Schuster and the author to continue publishing exceptional books for years to come. We thank you for supporting the author's copyright by purchasing an authorized edition of this book.
No amount of this book may be reproduced or stored in any format, nor may it be uploaded to any website, database, language-learning model, or other repository, retrieval, or artificial intelligence system without express permission. All rights reserved. Inquiries may be directed to Simon & Schuster, 1230 Avenue of the Americas, New York, NY 10020 or permissions@simonandschuster.com.
This book is a work of fiction. Any references to historical events, real people, or real places are used fictitiously. Other names, characters, places, and events are products of the author's imagination, and any resemblance to actual events or places or persons, living or dead, is entirely coincidental.
Text © 2025 by Gail Donovan
Jacket illustration © 2025 by Elysia Case
Jacket design by Karyn Lee
Interior illustration © 2025 by Elysia Case
All rights reserved, including the right of reproduction in whole or in part in any form.
ATHENEUM BOOKS FOR YOUNG READERS is a registered trademark of Simon & Schuster, LLC. Atheneum logo is a trademark of Simon & Schuster, LLC.
For information about special discounts for bulk purchases, please contact Simon & Schuster Special Sales at 1-866-506-1949 or business@simonandschuster.com.
Simon & Schuster strongly believes in freedom of expression and stands against censorship in all its forms. For more information, visit BooksBelong.com.
The Simon & Schuster Speakers Bureau can bring authors to your live event. For more information or to book an event, contact the Simon & Schuster Speakers Bureau at 1-866-248-3049 or visit our website at www.simonspeakers.com.
Interior design by Karyn Lee
The text for this book was set in Cotford Text.
The illustrations for this book were rendered digitally.
Manufactured in the United States of America
0925 BVG
First Edition
10 9 8 7 6 5 4 3 2 1
CIP data for this book is available from the Library of Congress.
ISBN 9781665963299
ISBN 9781665963312 (ebook)

For all the Sparrows
—G. D.

To all the animals in my life!
—E. C.

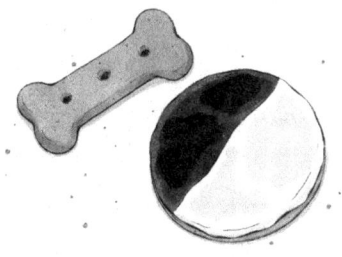

★ 1 ★

Sparrow was walking her kitten and searching for a bird, her face tilted up to the blue sky, which was why she wasn't paying attention to what was on the ground. Which was how she tripped on a tree root and landed splat on the sidewalk in front of a dog.

"Toby, sit," said the lady on the other end of the dog's leash. "Smart pup!" she added when he promptly sat. Then she asked Sparrow, "Are you okay?"

Sparrow scrambled from the ground. She had skinned her knee and scraped the palms of her hands. But who cared? The dog was gazing at her with shining brown eyes. It had short fur the color of honey and wore a blue guide-dog coat.

"I'm okay!" she said. "I'm totally okay."

"You took quite a tumble," said the lady.

Her voice was calm. Not calm and cold, like when a grown-up was trying not to scold. It was calm and warm, like the April afternoon. Her face had a calm look too. Even her long, straight black hair looked as if it never got tangled. Sparrow's hair got super tangled, and she hated having it brushed, which was why she always wore it in two braids.

"Your dog is so adorable. What kind is he?"

"This is Toby. He's a yellow Lab. One year old, so his body is full-grown, but he's still a puppy at heart."

At the end of her red leash, Sparrow's kitten, Gracie, was

staring at the dog. Sparrow knew what the kitten was feeling: curious. Gracie wanted to check out this Toby, just like Sparrow did. But Sparrow knew you weren't supposed to pet a guide dog. You weren't even supposed to ask. Gracie didn't know that, though. The black-and-white kitten was padding slowly toward the golden-furred dog. When she got closer, she looked up, and the dog looked down, and their noses touched.

"He's so good!" cried Sparrow.

"He needs to be," said the lady. "If he's going to be a guide dog, he needs to be able to handle situations like this."

Now Sparrow saw that Toby's blue coat said FUTURE GUIDE DOG. "So he's not one yet?"

"Not yet," said the lady. "Like I said, Toby's still a puppy, really, and I'm what they call a puppy raiser. I'm training him to be a well-behaved dog. In a couple of months he'll take a test to see if he can move up for his real guide dog training. Someone else will do that—if he passes the big test."

"I hate big tests," said Sparrow.

"Me too," admitted the lady. "School would be a lot more fun if there were no tests."

"A lot," agreed Sparrow. She used to love school. Sharing at Circle Time. Listening to books at Story Time. But fourth grade was starting to have a lot less sharing and stories and a lot more homework. And tests. And worst of all, group projects.

Toby was still sitting, like the lady had told him to, but Sparrow was sure he wanted her to pet him. He was gazing at her with his big brown eyes, which seemed to say, *Me three! I hate tests too! Pet me!* and his tail was kind of wagging. Since he was sitting down, it didn't wag very well, so it was more like thumping. Wag-thumping. Or thump-wagging.

Sparrow felt an answering thump in her heart. She couldn't pet the dog, though, no matter how much either of them wanted.

"What if he doesn't pass?"

"First the guide dog organization would see if he can do another kind of job. But if that doesn't work out, he could be adopted. The puppy raiser usually has first dibs, but I'd say no, so they'd find somebody else."

As Sparrow's mind soared straight to "somebody else" being her, she could almost hear her parents telling her not to get carried away. Not to get her hopes up, which was one of her least favorite things grown-ups said. What was so wrong about being hopeful? Except maybe she finally got the reason now. What was the point of hoping for something that could almost probably definitely never happen, and then being so sad when it didn't? For one thing, Toby might pass the test. And for another, she already had a kitten that she loved.

There was no way she could ever be the one to give Toby his forever home.

⤧ 2 ⤨

"Sorry for almost crashing into you," said Sparrow.

"It's really all right," said the lady. Toby was still sitting at her feet, like he was supposed to. The kitten had begun walking back and forth under the dog's chin, the white tip of her tail brushing his gold fur each time she slipped past. "I used to walk like that when I was a girl, not looking where I was going. My parents used to tell me to get my head out of the clouds."

"Mine say that to me!" said Sparrow.

Actually, Sparrow's mom and dad hardly said that anymore. They used to say she got too carried away. Or that she was being a drama queen. With her head in the clouds. They wanted her to rein it in. Dial it back. Come down to earth.

Then they took a class on parenting and started reading books, and began saying things that were basically the same idea but didn't sound quite so mean. And then they had another baby and didn't have so much time to work on fixing her. But Sparrow figured that sometime soon—when Asher stopped crying in the middle of the night—her parents would get back to trying to make her a little less Sparrow-the-way-she-was and a little more Sparrow-the-way-they-wanted-her.

"It seemed like you were looking for something," said the lady. "In the sky."

"My bird!" said Sparrow. "Well, not *my* bird. But a bird I know. She's a pigeon, and we named her Snowberry. She hit our window, and we took her to a place that fixed her wing, and when she was better, they brought her back here to let her go."

Together they looked up at the sky. A line of pigeons perched on the wires that swung from pole to pole along Hartley Street, too far away for Sparrow to tell if one of them was Snowberry.

It was late April in Maine, and spring was still arriving. The trees weren't bare winter brown anymore, but they weren't summer green yet either. They were in between. Some had bright lemon-lime-colored leaves, and others had caramel-colored leaves. But they were all just-getting-started leaves, like Asher's tiny baby hands curled into fists.

"Is that why you're walking your kitten on a leash? So it can't hurt birds?"

"Yes!" said Sparrow. "I don't think Gracie could catch one yet. But just in case."

"That's so responsible!" the lady said, and added, "And she's adorable."

That was true, in Sparrow's opinion. Gracie was black and white, like Sparrow's favorite cookie from the bakery on Bridge Street. Except Gracie's markings weren't divided evenly, like on the cookies. They were all jumbled up.

Sparrow launched into the story of how she'd gotten Gracie. Her family had moved here last summer, and Mrs. LaRose—she was the old lady who used to live in the other half of their house—had seven cats. Then Mrs. LaRose had to move out, and she could keep only one of her cats! Sparrow found new homes for the other six. And when the cat Mrs. LaRose was keeping turned out to be having kittens, Sparrow found homes for them, too. And got to keep one herself.

"Amazing Grace LaRose for long," she said, realizing as she wrapped up the story that it was probably way too much information. "Gracie for short."

But all the lady said was, "Wow, sounds like you really love animals."

"I do!" said Sparrow. "I love all animals. I love cats, especially Gracie cuz she's so soft and cuddly, but she's playful, too. And I love the way birds can fly. And we never had a dog, but I would love one so much. If it got along with Gracie, that is."

"Well, it looks like these two certainly get along," said the lady.

The kitten was still slinking back and forth under Toby's chin. He turned his face up toward Sparrow, his head tilted to one side with a quizzical look: *Is your kitten white with black splotches, or black with white splotches?* Which was what she could never decide!

"Do you think he's going to pass his test?"

"I hope so! I have a special feeling about Toby. I think he'd be great at guiding and that he'd love it. He's so eager—so enthusiastic. He wants to *go*."

Sparrow knew how that felt. "Eager" and "enthusiastic" were words for excited, which was how *she* got. She instantly changed her mind. She wasn't going to secretly wish she could give Toby his forever home, because that might jinx him. If Toby would love to be a guide dog, then that's what she wanted too.

"Me too!" she said. "I mean, I hope he passes too."

Now Toby's brown eyes seemed to say, *Me three! I hope I pass too!*

"It's been fun chatting," said the lady with a smile, "but I have to be somewhere, so I better get going." She pulled out her phone and glanced at it. "Actually, I think I'm already here. Eighty-seven Hartley."

"Eighty-seven Hartley?" asked Sparrow as she and the lady both looked at the house with the number 87 on the porch post. It was a white house with two front doors, both painted green.

"That's where *I* live!"

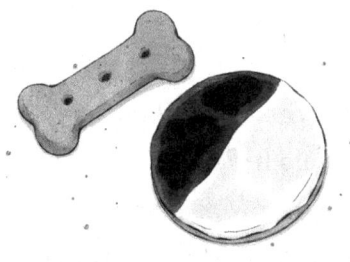

⤢ 3 ⤡

"This is not your decision to make, Sparrow," said her mom as she dropped two pieces of bread into the toaster.

Monday morning was not off to a good start. First, it was raining, which meant there would be indoor recess at school. Second, Sparrow was trying to talk to her parents. But they weren't listening. Maybe if she were as tall as them, they would pay more attention. She hopped up onto a kitchen chair. "But why can't we at least *talk* about it? Like, why *wouldn't* you rent the unit to that lady?"

Her parents both pointed to the floor.

"Floor!" said her mom.

"Floor!" said her dad.

Sparrow held out her arms and flew down off the chair.

"Sparrow, what have we said about climbing on the furniture?" asked her mom.

"That it was cute when I was little, but I'm too big for that now," recited Sparrow.

"That's right," said her mom.

"Now listen, Sparrow," said her dad. "To answer your question, we might rent the unit to the woman with the dog, and we might not. Someone else might be a better tenant."

"Better how?"

"Without a dog, for instance."

"What's wrong with having a dog? Toby is such a good dog! He's not going to do anything bad!"

"I have an idea," said Sparrow's mom. "How about we all take a breather?" She drew a deep breath to model "taking a calming breath," and Sparrow's dad did the same. The bread popped up from the toaster.

Sparrow sucked in some air and huffed it out as quickly as she could, pretending to breathe. She had to regular-breathe of course, but she wasn't special-breathing. She didn't want to calm down. She wanted to talk about Toby. "Well, when are you going to decide?"

"Here we go," said her mom, setting two pieces of toast on the table.

That was a nice thing about Asher, the baby. Her mom used to leave the house early for her job at a dentist's office, cleaning people's teeth, but now she was staying home for a while. Which meant that in the afternoons, Sparrow could come straight home from school. And in the mornings, *cinnamon toast*. Smeared with butter, sprinkled with cinnamon sugar, and cut into four triangles.

"*Yum,*" said Sparrow, biting into the first triangle.

"You're welcome," said her mom with a smile, before she bit into her own piece.

They were both cinnamon toast fans, which was kind of funny because they both had cinnamon-colored freckles sprinkled on their cheeks, along with light brown hair and brown eyes. Sparrow's dad had brown hair too, but his was darker. Plus, he had a mustache.

He sat down at the table with a cup of coffee. "Let's get things straight," he said. "How this is going to go."

Sparrow's dad was a big believer in getting things straight. He worked nights at a newspaper, fixing the stories other people wrote during the day. Making sure the grammar was right and that all the facts were correct. Between her dad being someone who made sure stories had no mistakes and her mom being someone who made sure teeth had no cavities, Sparrow sometimes felt like she didn't have a chance. They were fixers.

"Fact," said her dad. "Quite a few people answered the ad to rent the other half of our house. We're showing the unit to a few more people today. Then we'll make a decision."

"And we hear that you hope we'll decide to rent to the woman with the dog," added her mom, "whose name is Eileen Kim, by the way."

"And Toby," Sparrow reminded her. "So how will you decide?"

From the baby monitor on the kitchen counter came a faint squeaking sound. Asher was waking up.

"Mostly it will be whether we think they can pay the rent every month," said her dad. "We'll check their credit score. We'll check their references. It's grown-up stuff, Sparrow."

He didn't say *you wouldn't understand*, but he might as well have. Which made Sparrow mad. She *would* understand. They were the ones who didn't understand *her*. "All I want to know is, if she can pay the rent as good as anyone else—"

"As *well*," said her dad, interrupting her. "As well as anyone else."

Sparrow didn't get why kids interrupting grown-ups wasn't allowed, but grown-ups interrupting kids was. "Okay, but if she can pay the rent as *well* as anyone else, why wouldn't you let her have it? She's doing something really important! Toby's going to be a guide dog! You could be, like, helping someone get a guide dog!"

Asher's squeaks were getting louder.

"Time for somebody's second breakfast," said Sparrow's mom. "And, oh my gosh—it's way past time for you to go, Sparrow!"

"Want a ride?" asked her dad.

"No!" Maybe Sparrow wouldn't have minded a ride from her mom, but she knew her mom had to feed Asher. And she did not want a ride from her interrupting, grammar-correcting, you-wouldn't-understand dad. "I want to walk!"

"Let me get this straight," he said. "You want to walk in the rain and be late to school?"

"Yep," said Sparrow as she tugged on her rain boots. Then she slung on her backpack and headed out into the wet, gray day.

✧ 4 ✧

Walking to school in the rain, Sparrow decided that if April were a color, it would be yellow. The sky was gray, but everywhere something yellow was blooming. Yellow dandelions. Yellow daffodils. And big, shaggy bushes of yellow forsythia.

By the time she hurried through the doors of Eastbrook Elementary and speed-walked down the hallway, morning announcements were already on. *"Hot lunch is fish tacos; happy birthday to Samantha Ahmed; and there will be inside recess today."*

Sparrow stashed her raincoat in her locker. Inside her boots, her socks were wet from puddle-stomping on the way. And they had slipped down, so they were all wrinkled up under her feet. She hated that feeling. She didn't stop to fix it, though, because if she got to Mrs. Foxworthy's room before announcements finished, she wouldn't have to get a late pass from the office.

"*And now,*" said Principal Weiss, "*from all of us to all of you, welcome to school today!*"

Then came the recording of kids saying welcome in different languages: "*Bienvenidos. Ahlan wa sahlan.*" Mrs. Foxworthy had said that every year they made a new recording, and kids who knew another language could volunteer. Sparrow knew only English, but her best friend, Paloma, was going to volunteer for Spanish.

"*Bienvenue,*" came the last voice, right as Sparrow burst into Mrs. Foxworthy's fourth-grade classroom. She had made it!

Wait—*what?*

The blue pod—four desks pushed together, where she sat with Paloma and Anton and Caleb—was gone. All the pods were gone. All the desks were by themselves, in rows. Sparrow spotted the only empty one: right in the front row by the whiteboard. She made her way there, sat down, and twisted around in her seat to find Paloma's desk—miles away on the other side of the room. Paloma gave a little wave.

"Welcome, Sparrow!" said Mrs. Foxworthy. "I'm glad you're in time to hear me explain why the desks have been rearranged. To be honest, there's been a little too much chatting lately. And we have work to do! I want everyone to be ready for fifth grade. Fifth grade is important, because that's when you will really be getting ready for middle school."

Sparrow liked Mrs. Foxworthy. She wore red-framed eyeglasses that usually perched on her head in her short, spiky hair like a red bird in a nest. She wasn't too strict. And last fall she had even adopted one of Mrs. LaRose's cats that needed a home—the orange tabby named Marmalade.

But Sparrow did not like Mrs. Foxworthy's desk-moving idea. She couldn't believe her teacher was moving her desk *now* because of something that was years away. She tuned back in to hear "... and we'll be going to the library so you can begin researching your topic."

New research topics didn't sound horrible. Mrs. Foxworthy almost always let them pick their own because they were supposed to be self-directed learners. Sparrow knew exactly what she was going to pick. Guide dogs!

"And these," said Mrs. Foxworthy, holding up a stack of papers, "are your assignments."

Assigned topics? This day was not starting out so great. First, rearranged desks. Now assigned topics. Plus, wet socks.

Mrs. Foxworthy was walking up and down the rows of desks, handing out slips of paper. *Dogs,* wished Sparrow. *Please make it be dogs.*

Mrs. Foxworthy was getting closer. She dropped a slip of paper on Sparrow's desk.

Not dogs.

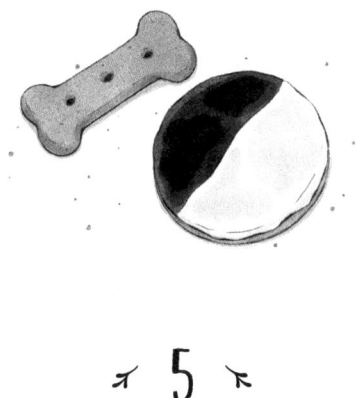

↗ 5 ↖

Sparrow had good reasons for not doing what she was supposed to do.

The class was supposed to be looking for books on their assigned topics in the library. But first she had to stop at her locker and take off her wet, wrinkled-under-her-feet socks. And then—because she hadn't been able to talk to Paloma all morning, since Mrs. Foxworthy had moved all the desks from pods into rows—she headed straight for their favorite spot in the school library, the beanbag nook. Paloma was already there, curled up on the pink beanbag with a pile of books beside her. Anton was there too, trying to build a tower with his stack of books.

Sparrow sank into the purple beanbag and wriggled around until the pellets were squished just right. "I got clouds," she grumbled. "What'd you get?"

"I got the moon," said Paloma.

"I got stormy weather!" said Anton. "Hurricanes! Tornadoes! So who would win? A hurricane or a tornado?"

"What does that even mean?" asked Paloma. "How would one of them *win*?"

"Like, would a hurricane beat a tornado, or would a tornado beat a hurricane," explained Anton. *"Duh."*

"But that doesn't even happen," argued Paloma. "They wouldn't be in a fight, like two animals might."

"Yeah, but if they did," pressed Anton.

This was how conversations with her two best friends almost always went, ever since the day Sparrow had met them. The first day of fourth grade.

She had instantly wanted to be friends with the girl wearing a kitty-cat headband in her thick, dark hair, who told Sparrow that she was named for a bird too! *Paloma* means "pigeon" or "dove" in Spanish. The amazing thing was they did get to be friends. Best friends. And when Sparrow got a kitty-cat headband too, Paloma never said Sparrow was copying. Paloma had even adopted one of the other kittens from Gracie's litter. And she had been at Sparrow's house the winter day that Snowberry crashed into the window, and together they had taken care of the bird until they could get her to a real bird rescue place.

Anton was Sparrow's second-best friend. He lived on Sparrow's street, and his mom ran a day care in her house, where Sparrow used to go for aftercare, so they had hung out a lot. They sang together in church choir, too. The good things about Anton were that he was funny, and he didn't care about boy-girl stuff. The not-good thing was that he could be kind of bouncy. Like on that first day of fourth grade, when he had asked who would win in a fight, a sparrow or a pigeon.

"Anton, we're still not playing 'Who would win?' with you," said Sparrow. "But what about the desks?"

"What about them?"

"The *rows*," said Sparrow. "Don't you hate them?"

"I guess," said Paloma. "But Mrs. Foxworthy says that's how they are in fifth grade."

"Yeah, but now we're not sitting together," said Sparrow.

"We can sit together at lunch," said Paloma, "and I'll see you at recess."

Sparrow stared at Paloma. She kind of couldn't believe what she was hearing. Except she kind of could, too. The good thing about Paloma was that she was easygoing. Happy to go along with what Sparrow wanted to do. But her easygoingness meant she also didn't mind stopping something and starting something else. She liked new things and changes. Sparrow liked things to stay the same. Or if something changed, she at least wanted a chance to check it out before she decided whether she liked it or not.

"Hey!" she said. Staring at Paloma, Sparrow had noticed something: Paloma wasn't wearing her kitty-cat headband. And now that Sparrow thought about it, she realized Paloma hadn't worn one for a while. Actually, Sparrow hadn't either, but that was because she'd lost hers, and her parents never seemed to get around to getting her a new one. "What happened to your cat ears?"

"I don't know," said Paloma with a shrug. "What happened to yours?"

"I lost them," said Sparrow.

"They're kind of babyish," said Paloma. "I don't think anyone wears them in fifth grade."

Everything suddenly felt like those drawings: *What's wrong with this picture?* One drawing had her and Paloma wearing their kitty-cat headbands, sitting together at the blue pod. The other drawing had them sitting miles apart, without their headbands. In the first picture they were best friends. In the second picture . . . Sparrow didn't know.

"Fourth graders!" called Mrs. Foxworthy. "We are heading back to our room in five minutes. Please make sure you've found enough books to begin researching your topic!"

"You better get some cloud books!" said Paloma. "Want me to help you look?"

"No, thanks," said Sparrow.

She clambered off the purple beanbag and headed for the stacks. She didn't need any help. And she didn't want books on clouds. She wanted books on dogs.

6

Back in the classroom, Sparrow tried reading the one book on clouds she had grabbed.

If she liked a book, she floated away into the world of the story. It felt like swimming. Or flying! But she didn't like the book on clouds. It was like all the words were so sticky. Like they were stuck to the page. "Stratus." "Cirrus." "Cumulus." They made Sparrow feel stuck too. Trapped. And Sparrow hated that feeling. It wasn't only that she didn't *want* to read about clouds. It felt like she *couldn't* read about clouds.

Sparrow slipped one of the books about dogs inside the book on clouds. That was better. She was deep into the chapter on the dog's daily workout when Mrs. Foxworthy called, "Listen up! I'm going to assign everyone their friendly feedback partner." She began listing off pairs of names.

Friendly feedback was when somebody told their partner what they had learned so far. Then the partner would listen and ask questions. What would they like to know more about? Was there anything confusing? Afterward they would use their partner's questions to keep working on their report. Sparrow didn't have a problem with friendly feedback. The problem was clouds.

Clouds, she thought. Nothing. She tried thinking the word faster. *Clouds clouds clouds.* Nope. Still nothing. She couldn't remember a single fact. Which was making her stomach begin to hurt. She was wondering about asking to go to the nurse's office when Yasmeen scooched her chair up to Sparrow's desk.

"We're partners!" said Yasmeen. "You want to go first?"

Sparrow liked Yasmeen, but they weren't good friends. Mostly because Sparrow was better at having one best friend than having lots of friends. She shook her head. "You can go first if you want."

"No, you!" insisted Yasmeen. Inside the circle her hijab made, she had a big smile on her face.

A few minutes later Mrs. Foxworthy wheeled her rolling stool alongside Sparrow's desk too. "Keep going," she said. "Don't mind me."

"Sparrow just finished!" volunteered Yasmeen. "And I

have a question and a comment. My question is: How does a guide dog learn to cross a street, like when cars are coming? And my comment is: That's so cool you're going to help somebody train a dog!"

There was a little silence then. Part of Sparrow wanted to explain that that wasn't *exactly* what she'd said. All she had said was that a lady who was training a guide dog named Toby *might* move into the other half of her house, and if she did, then *maybe* Sparrow could get to help. But even she knew this wasn't the right moment to correct Yasmeen.

Mrs. Foxworthy pulled her red glasses down from the top of her head to look at Sparrow's stack of books. One book on clouds. Seven books on dogs. Then she pushed her glasses back up on top of her head, gazing straight at Sparrow. Her face wasn't happy, obviously. But it wasn't mad, either. It was one of Sparrow's least favorite faces. The sad, disappointed-in-you face. Sparrow knew what that meant.

Trouble.

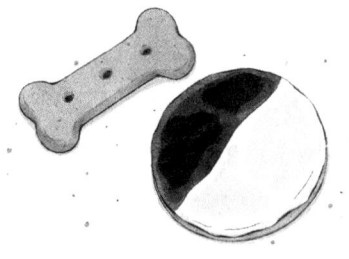

7

"Sparrow," said Mrs. Foxworthy, "did you have trouble finding material on clouds?"

"No, I saw the books on clouds," answered Sparrow, "but I only got this one."

"Because . . . ?"

"Because I really, really, *really* want to do my report on dogs."

"Dogs," said Mrs. Foxworthy.

"Yes!" said Sparrow. "Actually, not just any kind of dog. I want to study guide dogs, because this lady I know—well, this lady who's going to move into the other half of my house . . . well, I mean I *hope* she is—she has a guide dog. So I want to know everything I can about guide dogs. Just in case. So could I switch?"

"I'm sorry," said Mrs. Foxworthy, shaking her head, so

her red glasses swung back and forth. "No, that doesn't work."

Why did people say "sorry" when they weren't sorry? Mrs. Foxworthy didn't sound sorry at all!

"Sparrow, I know you can learn about something you're interested in. But this wasn't free choice. This was an assignment. I've been noticing that's a pattern with your work. If you aren't interested in something, you don't do your best work."

Sparrow couldn't help that! Mrs. Foxworthy was going on and on. Knowing how to study. Paying attention and following directions. Getting ready for fifth grade.

Fifth grade, fifth grade, fifth grade. It was like Mrs. Foxworthy was obsessed with fifth grade! Suddenly Sparrow had a scary thought. At least now she and Paloma were still in the same class. But what about next year? What if they weren't in the same fifth-grade class? Sparrow twisted around in her seat, trying to catch Paloma's attention. But she was so far away. It was like Mrs. Foxworthy had put them as far apart as possible!

"*Sparrow!*" said Mrs. Foxworthy. "Listening means looking at the person who is speaking. Can you look at me, please?"

Sparrow turned back to Mrs. Foxworthy.

"Did you hear what I said?"

Sparrow didn't know. Something about fifth grade probably.

"I know!" piped up Yasmeen. "You said everyone needs to know about their topic, so you don't let down your classmates in the group project." She gave Sparrow a big smile.

Nice! thought Sparrow, grinning back at Yasmeen.

"Thank you, Yasmeen," said Mrs. Foxworthy. "But I wanted to hear from Sparrow."

By now the whole class was tuning in to hear what Sparrow would say next. But the way Mrs. Foxworthy was talking made Sparrow's head feel like she'd eaten ice cream too fast. Like her brain was frozen. Actually, her whole *self* felt frozen! Like she was frozen stuck in this miles-from-Paloma chair. And she hated feeling stuck!

Mrs. Foxworthy drew a big being-patient breath. "Let's try this again, Sparrow. You may go back to the library to find more books on your assigned topic."

"Right now?"

"Right now."

Finally! Sparrow couldn't wait to get up from her new miles-from-Paloma, stuck-in-the-corner seat. She pushed back her chair, stood up, and walked away.

At the doorway she heard Mrs. Foxworthy call her name and the one-word reminder—"Chair!"—but she didn't go back to tuck in her chair. She kept right on going.

⊀ 8 ⊁

It rained all week. On Saturday morning the sun came out, and so did Sparrow and her family. Her mom and dad sat on the top step of the porch with their cups of coffee, and Asher between them in his bouncy seat. Holding Gracie on her leash, Sparrow stood on the lawn. The sun after all the rain had made a new crop of yellow dandelions spring out of the grass, like those just-add-water sponge toys.

"Me and Gracie are going for a walk," said Sparrow. Though "walk" was not really the right word. Sparrow had found out you didn't really walk a cat. You went for a walk-pause-sit, walk-pause-sit. Repeat. In slow motion.

"Sparrow, wait a sec," called her dad.

"*Sorry,*" she groaned. "Gracie and *I* are going for a walk."

"Oh, good catch! But that's not it. We need to talk to you." There was something in the sound of his voice that said,

Wait for it. Like whatever he had to say wasn't about grammar. Like it was something good.

"We have some news about the unit," said her mom.

"Miss Kim was the best candidate," said her dad.

"So we're renting the unit to her," finished her mom.

Sparrow felt like she had to spring out of the grass like a dandelion too. She scooped up Gracie in her arms and took off, racing in a circle around the big maple in their front yard and back to the porch, where her parents sat with big smiles on their faces. Sparrow wanted Asher to smile too. She zipped up the steps, zoomed in toward her baby brother, and made a funny face, trying to coax a smile. Paloma, who had a little brother, had shown her how. First Sparrow made big chipmunk cheeks, and then she squirted out the air to make a funny noise. Asher didn't smile, though. He looked surprised. Then he burst into a little gurgling laugh.

"His first laugh!" cried her mom.

"Well done, Sparrow!"

Sparrow sat down beside her mom. She liked this feeling. Perched on the porch steps with Gracie in her lap and her family all around. Everyone happy. Everything warm and sunny. Even Gracie's fur was warm in the sun. Sparrow ran her hand around the curve of the kitten's back, going from splotch to splotch like connect the dots.

"Sparrow," said her mom. "There's something else we need to talk about too." The sound of her voice didn't have a fun wait-for-it feeling. It felt more like clouds covering the sun. "Your dad and I had a meeting with Mrs. Foxworthy. On Zoom. She told us how you didn't follow directions. She asked you to tuck in your chair, and you walked away."

"Wait—*what?*" spluttered Sparrow. "She's mad I didn't tuck in my *chair?*"

"She's not mad at you, Sparrow," said her dad. "She was concerned by how distressed you seemed about the new desk layout, and by how you were unable to focus on your work."

"Can you tell us what happened right before the chair thing?" asked her mom.

"All I said was that I wished I could do my report on guide dogs instead of clouds!" explained Sparrow. "Because I wanted to know everything there is about guide dogs, because maybe Toby was going to move in. And I was thinking that if he moved in, maybe I could—you know—help him learn to be a guide dog. But not if I don't know anything!"

"Sparrow, Sparrow, Sparrow," said her dad, shaking his head. "You think you might be getting a little carried away?"

"Not really," she said, "because Toby *is* moving in!"

"I meant the part about you helping. That's not your job. Your job is being in fourth grade, and getting ready for fifth grade."

"Yes, let's get back to that," said Sparrow's mom. "Mrs. Foxworthy had a great idea."

Sparrow was not a fan of great ideas. In her experience, they were usually things like joining the church choir, taking swimming lessons, or everybody chipping in to tidy the house for fifteen minutes (which always ended up lasting an hour).

"She thinks you could benefit from taking part in a friendship group."

"A what?"

"A friendship group," explained her mom. "It's a small pullout group that meets every other day during lunch. With Mrs. Kosanovich, the social worker, and a few other kids."

"I can't!" said Sparrow. "Lunch is the only time I have to see Paloma! Mrs. Foxworthy moved our desks a mile apart! Did she tell you *that*?"

Sparrow's dad chimed in with a few fact-straighteners. "It's not every day, Sparrow. It's only Mondays, Wednesdays, and Fridays. So on Tuesdays and Thursdays you can still eat with Paloma. And you can see her at recess."

Why did her dad think that straightening out the facts would make her feel better? Facts weren't the point! The point was that all she wanted was to sit with Paloma in class and at lunch. And to learn about guide dogs. Why couldn't her parents figure that out?

"Sparrow," said her mom, "you know Mrs. Foxworthy is only trying to help, right?"

"Yeah, but I don't need any help!" said Sparrow.

Sparrow's mom drew a deep breath, then said, "Let's review. What happened when Mrs. LaRose had to move and couldn't keep her cats?"

"I found homes for them."

"And what did Mrs. Foxworthy do?"

"She took Marmalade."

It was true that when Sparrow had been searching for homes for Mrs. LaRose's cats, her teacher had taken the orange tabby. So, yes, Mrs. Foxworthy had helped her. Except that help wasn't really for *her*. It was for the cats!

"And what about Snowberry?"

It was true that when the pigeon had flown into Sparrow's bedroom window and hurt her wing, she and Paloma had put the bird in a quiet place with birdseed and water, hoping it would get better. When it didn't, she had to ask her uncle Chris to help get Snowberry to a bird sanctuary. But that help wasn't really for *her*! It was for Snowberry.

"Uncle Chris helped me take Snowberry to Sunny Skies."

"So what does that tell you?"

"I know, I know! I didn't help the cats and Snowberry all by myself. People helped me. But I don't need any help now, and I don't need any new friends, so why do I need to go to friendship group?"

Before her parents could answer, a car pulled up in front of the house, and Miss Kim and Toby got out.

9

Ten minutes later Sparrow took a sip of lemonade. It was sweet and sour and made her whole mouth feel zingy.

"It's not quite lemonade weather yet," said Sparrow's mom, pouring another glass and handing it to Miss Kim, "but when we moved in, our landlady welcomed us with lemonade. Now that we own the house, we wanted to do the same."

They were all sitting around Sparrow's family's kitchen table, except for Asher, who was back in his crib, taking a nap. Gracie was curled up on Sparrow's lap, and Toby sat on the floor beside Miss Kim's chair. He had a goofy look on his face, with his head tilted to one side and his tongue hanging out of his mouth.

"So," said Sparrow's dad, raising his glass, "welcome to Hartley Street!"

"*Bienvenue!*" piped up Sparrow. "That's what Mrs. LaRose said!"

"That's French!" said Miss Kim, turning to Sparrow with a big smile on her face. "Do you speak French?"

"Not really," said Sparrow. "All I know is *bonjour* and *bienvenue* and *oui*. And *c'est la vie!*"

"'Hello,' 'welcome,' 'yes,' 'that's life!'" said Miss Kim. "That's a good start!" She wore blue jeans and a shirt the same blue as Toby's vest, with white polka dots. Pulled back in a clip, her long black hair showed a single thick streak of white, like the Milky Way in the night sky.

Sparrow had seen pictures of the Milky Way because Paloma had gotten assigned the moon, so she was in the Solar System group. Sparrow had gotten clouds, so she was in Weather. She didn't want to think about school, though. She took another zing of lemonade and tuned back in to the grown-ups' conversation. It was getting-to-know-you stuff. Miss Kim was from Vermont, where her parents were both teachers; her mom taught English literature and her dad taught Korean; and she was a civil engineer. Sparrow's mom asked what that was, exactly.

"To be honest, I spend most of my day thinking about water. Let's say there's a building. My job is to design everything around it. I try to make sure water moves in the right direction—away from the building, not inside it."

The grown-ups kept talking. They had a ridiculous amount to say about water. How it could come down through the roof or up from the basement. How you tried to keep it out but you couldn't always stop it. Then you had to get it out as soon as possible.

Sparrow began wiggle-waggling the tip of her braid for Gracie. As Gracie reached up a paw to bat the braid, the kitten's tail began swishing back and forth. Sitting beside them, Toby began flicking his honey-gold head back and forth too, following Gracie's tail.

Sparrow stopped for a second. Gracie's tail stopped, and so did Toby's head. She tried it again. She wiggle-waggled her braid, Gracie swished her tail, and Toby flicked his head. Stop. And again. Wiggle-waggle, swish, flick.

"Look at you!" said Miss Kim. "You really get them!" She turned to Sparrow's parents. "I need to tell you how impressed I am with Sparrow and how she behaves around

Toby. Most kids would ask to pet him, and she hasn't. Not the day we met on the sidewalk, and not today."

"That's so sweet of you to say," said Sparrow's mom, and her dad added, "Sparrow's an animal lover, for sure. She really connects with them."

Sparrow wanted to ask about Toby's test that was coming up. "Miss Kim—"

"Oh gosh! You can call me Eileen."

Sparrow looked at her mom to see what she should do. Her parents were big on manners, which meant no first names for grown-ups. "Miss Eileen," prompted her mom, and Miss Kim—Miss Eileen now—nodded and said, "That works." She might be impressed with Sparrow, but she was still on the grown-up team.

Sparrow started again. "Miss Eileen, how much longer until Toby's test?"

"A little over a month, on June eleventh."

"That's my birthday!" said Sparrow. "I'm nine going on ten."

"Ooh, the double-digit birthday! That's a big one." Miss Eileen placed her hand on Toby's big, blocky head, and he laid his chin on her leg, his tail wag-thumping the floor.

Sparrow felt the answering thump in her heart again. She had changed her mind about wishing she could adopt him. But she still wished that she could pat him and he would half wag, half thump his tail like that. And she didn't care if this was getting carried away—she wished she could help Toby get to be a guide dog!

Suddenly she felt a soft nudge—Gracie bumping her head against Sparrow's hand: *Pet me.* Sparrow felt a quick flick of guilt. While she had been thinking and talking about Toby, she had stopped playing with the kitten. Patting her now, she made a silent promise. No matter what, she was always going to love Gracie. Obviously!

"This has been so nice," said Miss Eileen, "but I should get going. Before I go, though, I have a question for Sparrow. It's good for Toby to get used to working with different people besides me. So how would you like to help by coming along on some walks? If it's okay with your parents, that is."

10

Sparrow scooped up a spoonful of blueberry from the bottom of her yogurt cup, swirling purple and white together to turn it all lavender.

"I'm Mrs. Kosanovich," said the social worker. "But please call me Mrs. K."

Sparrow's parents had offered her a deal. There was no getting out of going to friendship group. The deal was that if she could "be a cooperator"—which meant going along without making a big getting-carried-away fuss about it—she could help walk Toby. So here she was. But that didn't mean she had to like it. She dipped her spoon into her cup and swallowed a mouthful of blueberry yogurt.

"Who knows the getting-to-know-you game two truths and a lie?" Mrs. K. raised her own hand to model raising your hand, and the silver bangles on her wrist slid down her arm. She wore a teal-colored dress, and her sneakers were teal too. Even her short silver-gray hair was dotted with streaks of teal.

Sparrow raised her hand. So did the three other kids. There were two girls Sparrow didn't know, both named Isla. They looked almost exactly alike, with white skin and long, straight blond hair. The only difference was one of them wore her hair in a single ponytail, and the other in two pigtails. Sparrow dubbed them Isla One and Isla Two.

The other kid was a boy named Orion. Sparrow knew him a little but not a lot. He was in Mrs. Foxworthy's class too, and sometimes he played clapping games with the girls at recess. But Sparrow and Orion had never really talked. Orion was wearing what Sparrow's dad would call "church clothes"—a plaid shirt with collar and buttons. He had super-curly sandy-brown hair and sat with his arms crossed and his legs swinging, so his feet kept bumping against the chair legs.

"Great!" said Mrs. K. "I'll go first. My favorite color is teal. My favorite ice cream is mocha chip. And my dream is to go skydiving. Who wants to go next?"

"I don't want to," said Orion. "Do I have to?"

"Nope," said Mrs. K. "But I'll ask you to think about going next time, okay? How about you, Sparrow?"

Time to "be a cooperator." Sparrow decided to make the lie be the middle thing. "My favorite cookie is the black-and-white. My middle name is Amanda. And I'm gonna help train a puppy to be a guide dog."

"I bet that's the lie!" blurted Orion, pointing at Sparrow. "She told our class she had seven cats, and it totally wasn't true."

"It's not a lie!" cried Sparrow. Way back in the beginning of fourth grade, she had told Mrs. Foxworthy's class she had seven cats. But later she had apologized and told them the truth: they were her neighbor's cats she was helping take care of. "And I *said* I was *sorry*!"

"I'm going to ask all of us to take a breath," said Mrs. K. She drew a deep breath and slowly blew it out.

Isla One and Isla Two did the same, taking long, noisy breaths. Orion kept bouncing his feet on the legs of his chair. Breathing, obviously, but not making a big deal about it. It looked as if he didn't like being told to breathe any more than Sparrow did.

Mrs. K. asked, "Who can remind us how we can have more fun when we play a game?"

Isla One piped up, "Wait your turn."

"Waiting your turn," agreed Mrs. K. "I know how hard that can be. And I know it's hard when somebody thinks something about you that isn't true." She paused to smile at Sparrow, then went on. "A lot of things in life can feel hard. That's something we'll spend some time on here, talking about what to do when that happens. Now, does anyone want to guess my lie?"

"Your favorite color is teal," said Isla One.

"Nope," said Mrs. K., shaking her head, with its streaks of teal.

"Your favorite ice cream is mocha chip!" tried Isla Two.

"Nope. Skydiving—which I do *not* want to try—was my lie. But let me tell you why I love the color teal and the flavor mocha chip. Something that's hard for me is making up my mind. Since teal is blue and green, and mocha chip is coffee and chocolate—"

"And chocolate chips!" interrupted Isla One.

"And chocolate chips," agreed Mrs. K. "Since teal and mocha chip are blends of two things I like, I don't have to choose. So that's my little work-around." She glanced at the silver watch on her wrist. "I am so sorry, but we need to stop for today. Whoever didn't get a turn can go next time. And we'll talk more about other work-arounds and strategies for what to do when things feel hard. See you Wednesday!"

Sparrow tossed her empty yogurt container in the trash and headed out the door. Mrs. K. wasn't actually too bad. And Isla One and Isla Two were okay. But one thing Sparrow knew for sure. Just because they called this friendship group did not mean she was going to be friends with Orion. That was not going to happen.

11

Sparrow raced home from school, dropped her backpack, gave her mom a quick "hi-bye," then bolted back out the door. Took five giant steps along the front porch. Knocked on the other door.

"First things first," said Miss Eileen, after letting Sparrow inside. "When we're walking outside, Toby will be on duty. But right now, while we're inside, he's only a dog. Off duty. Go ahead and pat him."

"Really?" cried Sparrow.

"Really," said Miss Eileen.

Finally! Toby lay in the middle of a braided rug. Sparrow sank down beside him, reached her hand out to the top of his honey-gold head, and ran it down along his back. And again. Toby's tail began thump-wagging, and Sparrow felt like she was in the exact right place. Doing the exact right thing. It felt like sliding into a pond on a summer day. Or slipping under the covers as your mom tucked you in.

"He likes you!" said Miss Eileen.

"Doesn't he like everybody?"

"Well, kind of. He's a lovebug, for sure."

"You're a lovebug," Sparrow told Toby.

As she talked to Miss Eileen, she stopped patting Toby for a second, and he gave her a *Pet me!* nudge, like Gracie sometimes did. Unlike Gracie, he also gave her a big, slobbery lick of his tongue. "Toby, that tickles!"

She began patting him again, and he flopped onto his side, then rolled onto his back, paws up in the air. Sparrow looked up at Miss Eileen, checking, because it seemed like Toby wanted her to keep patting him, but she wasn't sure. That was the one place Gracie didn't always like to be patted—her stomach.

Miss Eileen gave her a big smile. "It's great that you know to wait and see. Dogs give signals about how they're feeling, just like people do. See how his tongue is hanging out, and he's kind of wriggling? That tells us he's happy and relaxed, and he'd welcome a belly rub."

"You're a lovebug who wants a tummy rub," said Sparrow, patting Toby's belly while his paws wiggle-waggled in the air.

"Look how happy he is!" said Miss Eileen. "He loves kids. The next few weeks are going to be a nice time for him to just be a dog and spend time with you. If you want to, that is."

"I do!" said Sparrow.

"I'm kidding. I know you do."

Toby's eyes began drooping closed.

"Is he going to sleep?" asked Sparrow.

"No, he's just super relaxed. He gets the difference between on duty and off duty. On duty, he's ready to go. Off duty, he's ready to snooze."

"I'll snooze with you, Toby, if you want," said Sparrow as she lay down on the braided rug and snuggled up alongside the dog.

"Aw, you're snug as two bugs in a rug."

"Snug as two lovebugs in a rug!" said Sparrow.

Miss Eileen laughed. "All right, you two lovebugs. You can snooze another day. Now it's time for something called 'Get busy.'"

Guide dogs weren't supposed to pee or poop while they were guiding, she explained. So first you took them outside and gave them the command to go to the bathroom. She clipped the leash on Toby and opened the door, and Sparrow followed them outside.

"Get busy!" said Miss Eileen.

Toby began sniffing the grass, looking for the perfect spot. When he found it, he squatted to poop.

Sparrow didn't want to see *that*! She looked away, up at the blue sky.

"Okay," announced Miss Eileen a minute later. "This is not the fun part. But it's part of the job." She held out a plastic bag. "Want to try scooping some poop?"

⚞ 12 ⚟

There had been a lot of discussion of poop in Sparrow's house lately. "Has Asher pooped?" "What a poopy diaper!" But Sparrow hadn't had to do anything about it! Her mom and dad changed diapers, not her! Now she looked down at the green grass and the yellow dandelions. And the brown poop. She put her hand in the bag and reached down—ugh, it was warm, and even though she was holding her breath, it still smelled!—and scooped up the poop.

"Well done!" said Miss Eileen. She put the blue FUTURE GUIDE DOG vest on Toby. "We only put the vest on after 'Get busy.' The vest signals to the dog that it's time to work now."

"He looks different," observed Sparrow. "Excited! Like he knows he's going to do something important."

"Isn't that neat?" asked Miss Eileen. "The vest makes a dog sort of stand up straight and tall, you know? He knows he's on duty now."

She went on to explain that all puppy raisers used the same basic commands: "Sit," "Down," "Close," "Stand," and "Come." When a dog did what was asked, it got a reward. For younger puppies that meant food. But the older a puppy got, the less you used kibble treats and the more you used a verbal reward.

"That can be anything you want, like 'Yay for you!' or 'Aren't you a clever puppy!'"

They started off down Hartley Street then, with Miss Eileen walking Toby.

Sparrow had pictured herself walking Toby. Now she realized she wasn't sure exactly what Miss Eileen had meant by "help." Maybe she had only meant that Sparrow could come along while she walked Toby. But then why had she said "it's part of the job" when she asked if Sparrow wanted to scoop Toby's poop?

Sparrow wondered if this was some kind of test. Was she supposed to be patient—one of her least favorite things—and wait until Miss Eileen asked her if she wanted to walk Toby? Which of course she did! But before Sparrow had time to ask, Miss Eileen said, "Uh-oh!"

In the distance someone was walking toward them with a dog on a leash, their arm stretched straight out as the dog tugged them forward, barking the whole time.

Miss Eileen stopped and asked Toby to sit. Toby sat. "Smart pup!" she said to the dog, and to Sparrow, "What shall we do here? Any ideas?"

"Um, cross the street?"

"Excellent idea!"

They crossed, and as they set off walking again, Miss Eileen talked about how "distance is your friend." How if you ever came across something that could be a problem, a good strategy was simply to give it some distance. A puppy raiser's job was to help their dog have basic good-dog manners and a positive experience so that he was ready for the test.

"What about if the person Toby is guiding wants to cross the street, but there's a car coming?" Sparrow asked.

"Great question! There's something called intelligent disobedience. Toby will have to know that sometimes he needs to make a decision *not* to do what he was told to do. That's a super-advanced skill the real trainer will teach Toby during harness training."

"If he passes the test," said Sparrow.

"If he passes the test," agreed Miss Eileen.

"On my birthday!"

"That's right. So, do you know what you want for your birthday?"

Now that Sparrow had gotten to pat Toby, there was only one thing she wanted, and it wasn't a present that someone could put in a box and wrap up in paper. "It's not really a *thing*," she explained, "but I wonder—you know how you said I could help by coming along on some walks?"

Miss Eileen nodded.

"Does that mean . . . could I ever—you know—be the one to hold the leash?"

⚲ 13 ⚰

The good news was that when Sparrow asked if she could ever actually walk Toby, Miss Eileen didn't say no. And she didn't say "We'll see," which was technically better than no, but Sparrow still hated it. She said, "Yes, someday." "Someday" wasn't Sparrow's favorite—she would rather know exactly when—but it wasn't terrible.

The next day was the same as the first. Sparrow scooped Toby's poop, then Miss Eileen walked Toby. They went in the same direction down Hartley Street, walking past five houses. Then turned around and came back.

Third day, same deal, same route. Poop scooping and following along.

The next day, after "Get busy," Miss Eileen put Toby's blue FUTURE GUIDE DOG vest on him, and Toby seemed to stand up a little straighter. Then she turned to Sparrow and held out the leash. "Ready to try?"

"Yes!" cried Sparrow. She took the leash in her hand, feeling like she was standing up a little straighter now too. Just like Toby.

"Before we start, you need to pick your verbal reward. Remember? What you'll say when Toby does what you ask?"

Sparrow thought for a second. "Can mine be 'Good job, lovebug!'?"

"Excellent choice," said Miss Eileen with a smile. "I like it."

They set off down Hartley Street. It had been two weeks since Sparrow first met Miss Eileen and Toby. April had turned into May, and all the trees had changed. Their lemon-lime leaves used to be curled up like tiny baby fists. Now all the leaves had opened up and turned a deeper green. They seemed to be waving at Sparrow, up in the sky. Higher up in the sky hung the big, fluffy clouds called cumulus.

I could put that in my cloud journal, thought Sparrow as they walked along. Same route as always. Same two people and one dog.

But this time Sparrow was walking the dog.

14

That Sunday was the best day of Sparrow's life.

First, Miss Eileen decided to go to church with them, and she took Toby along. The youth choir was singing, so instead of having Sunday school, Sparrow got to march into the service with Anton and the other choir kids, wearing a long purple robe. They sang "Simple Gifts" and "Amazing Grace." And even though people weren't supposed to clap in church because it wasn't a show, everybody clapped.

Second, on the way home Miss Eileen let Sparrow walk Toby all the way up Hartley Street. The world was bright with color. Cumulus clouds sailing across a bright blue sky. Red cardinals darting here and there. Yellow things blooming. Green grass.

Third, Miss Eileen told Sparrow's parents that she had done fantastic last week with Toby.

"We did three days with me showing her what to do, then three days with her doing it. And she passed the poop-scoop test with flying colors. So I have an idea." She wondered if Sparrow would like to try walking Toby by herself after school.

"By myself?" cried Sparrow. "Yes!"

"Wow," said Sparrow's dad. "Sounds like a big responsibility."

"Which is a great thing to learn," Sparrow's mom reminded him.

"That's true," he admitted.

Miss Eileen went on. "I can keep working from home in the afternoons, so I'd be around, of course. And I'd have her walk the exact same route we did every day last week."

Sparrow's mom asked, "So she could be kind of like a mother's helper?"

"Yes!" said Miss Eileen. "Like I said, it can be good for a dog to work with different people. Toby knows what to expect with me. This will give him a chance to be a good dog with somebody else."

Sparrow's parents were quiet for a little bit as they walked along. Not saying yes yet but not saying no, either.

Sparrow kept quiet too. Walking. Waiting. Hoping. And not even reminding them how she had gone along with friendship group like they wanted! But right then they got to the house, so she said something. "Toby, sit."

Toby sat, then gave a quick twist of his head to look back at her with his big brown eyes. Like he was saying, *Are you so proud of me?*

"Good job, lovebug!" she said.

"And good job, Sparrow," said Miss Eileen, taking the leash.

Sparrow's mom and dad were looking at each other with *What do you think? No, what do you think?* faces. That turned into smiling faces. Which was why this day turned into the best day of Sparrow's life.

Followed by the worst.

⤧ 15 ⤦

Today wasn't supposed to be the worst day of Sparrow's life. Today was supposed to be another best day. After school Paloma was coming over for a playdate. Sparrow was going to show her Toby, and then she was going to walk him all by herself. Herself and Paloma!

But before she got to after school there was school, and Mrs. Foxworthy announcing it was time. They'd been studying their assigned topics on their own for the last two weeks. Now it was time to put their learning together. Time to start working in groups.

Half the class was in Solar System. Their group was so big, the teacher's aide was taking them to another room to work. Sparrow watched as Paloma walked out, followed by Anna, Serenity, Henry, Owen, and Ahmed. Then came a few stragglers and finally Orion, bringing up the rear.

The other half of the class was divided into two smaller groups: the Water Cycle and Weather. Sparrow and the other Weather kids went to sit at the low, round table in the corner.

"Let's all go around and say what type of weather we are," suggested Harriet. "I'm sunshine."

"Clouds," said Sparrow.

"Rain," said Yasmeen.

"Wind," said Caleb.

"Best for last," boasted Anton. "I'm stormy weather!"

"Now we have to figure out some way to, like, *present* weather," said Harriet. "You know. Talk about it. Show it."

Harriet was wearing a shirt that matched her perfectly, Sparrow thought, with a picture of a bee and the words "Queen Bee" spelled out in sequins. Sparrow didn't mind Harriet being bossy, though. Somebody had to be in charge. The rest of the group was pretty good too.

Yasmeen. She had been nice to Sparrow during friendly feedback, when Mrs. Foxworthy found out Sparrow had been reading books on dogs instead of clouds. Caleb. He had taken one of her neighbor's cats that needed a home last fall. And Anton. Anton was Anton. Wild card.

"Who has an idea?" asked Harriet.

Sparrow looked around to see if anyone else wanted to go first. Across the room, Mrs. Foxworthy was talking to the Water Cycle kids.

"I could do a poster with cotton balls," offered Sparrow. "Like for the wispy ones—they're called cirrus—I can pull them apart. And I can pile them up for the puffy ones. They're called cumulus. I saw some when I was walking Toby. He's a guide dog. Well—a future guide dog. I walk him after school."

"No way!" said Harriet, who didn't seem to mind going from weather to dogs. "If I was blind, I would have a guide dog named Topaz."

"You might not get to name it," said Caleb, who also didn't seem to mind changing the subject. "They probably already come with a name. Like my cat, Tuxedo."

"You're so lucky!" said Yasmeen. "Is it fun?"

Sparrow nodded. "Except for when you start, you have to scoop their poop."

"*What?*" cried Anton.

Sparrow explained the whole "Get busy" concept. "First you say, 'Get busy,' and then he poops, and then you—you know—put it in a bag."

"*Gross!*" crowed Anton. "You mean you *picked it up*?"

"In a *bag!*" said Sparrow. "It's no big deal." She actually felt like it was a big deal. But she wasn't sure she liked Anton making it a big deal.

"No big deal," agreed Caleb. "She's a poop scooper."

Anton got a happy look on his face. Bouncing a little in his seat, he chanted, "Poop scooper, poop scooper."

"Quit it, Anton," warned Sparrow. "It's not funny!"

Anton didn't quit. "Sparrow is a poop scooper," he said in a singsong voice.

"Sparrow is a poop scooper," echoed Caleb.

"Caleb should quit too," pointed out Yasmeen.

Neither of them was quitting, though.

"Sparrow is a poop scooper," said Anton, "busy scooping puppy poop."

"Busy scooping puppy poop," said Caleb, "from a super-poopy puppy!" which made Anton laugh so hard, he almost fell off his chair. Then Caleb gave him a helping push, and Anton landed on the floor, still laughing.

Sparrow sensed Mrs. Foxworthy's eyes on them. "Get up!" she snapped. She gave him a nudge with her foot. "You're going to get us all in trouble!"

"Quit kicking me!" cried Anton.

Sparrow was already mad, and being accused of something she hadn't done made her even madder. She hadn't kicked Anton! She had only nudged him.

"*That* wasn't a kick," she said. Then she stomped on his foot. "*That* was."

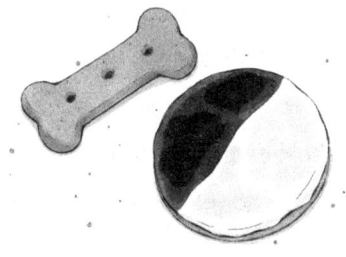

16

Mrs. Foxworthy seemed to fly across the room. Without a word, she pointed to Anton's empty chair. He scrambled up from the floor and took his seat. Next, Mrs. Foxworthy pointed at Harriet. "Harriet. What's going on here?"

"Sparrow was telling us about her dog," began Harriet, "and Anton and Caleb started teasing about, um . . ." She trailed off. She didn't want to get in trouble herself.

"Poop!" volunteered Yasmeen, coming to Sparrow's defense. "They were totally teasing!"

Sparrow shot Yasmeen a grateful smile as Mrs. Foxworthy put both hands together, in prayer position, and closed her eyes for a second, like she was praying that when she opened them, she wouldn't be here anymore. She opened her eyes and looked straight at Sparrow.

"Sparrow. Working in a group means respecting one

another. When you talk about something that isn't part of the assignment, you're not respecting your classmates."

Sparrow could not believe how unfair this was. And she hated when things weren't fair. She *had so* talked about the assignment, and she'd even had an idea for a poster! "Anton wasn't respectful when he teased me about poop scooping!" she cried.

"Well, you didn't have to kick me!" he blurted.

There was a hold-your-breath silence as everyone waited to see what would happen now that Anton had told on Sparrow.

Mrs. Foxworthy turned to Anton. "Anton, I'm going to ask you a question, and I want you to answer in one word: yes or no. Were you teasing Sparrow?"

"Yes," said Anton.

"Can you apologize?"

"Sorry," said Anton cheerfully.

That was easy for Anton to say. He should be sorry!

"Thank you, Anton," said Mrs. Foxworthy. She turned back to Sparrow. "I'm going to ask you a question, Sparrow, and I want you to answer in one word: yes or no. Did you kick Anton?"

Sparrow wasn't going to lie. "Yes," she said.

"And?" prompted Mrs. Foxworthy.

That was another thing Sparrow hated: when grown-ups tried to make you apologize. Even if you weren't sorry, they still wanted you to say it.

Sparrow sat with her hands clenched in her lap as everyone looked at her. Waiting.

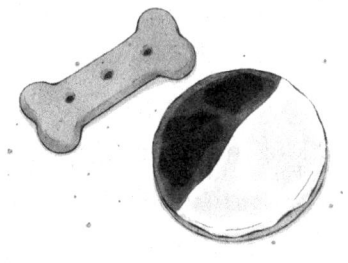

⚹ 17 ⚹

No matter how long Mrs. Foxworthy stared down at Sparrow with her sad, disappointed-in-you face, it wasn't going to happen.

Mrs. Foxworthy wanted Sparrow to apologize. Not only for stomping on Anton's foot, which probably hardly even hurt him, but okay, she knew she should apologize for that. But no. Mrs. Foxworthy also wanted Sparrow to apologize for not respecting all the Weather group kids and the work they were doing. But Sparrow hadn't disrespected anybody! Everybody else had wanted to talk about Toby too! So even if she said the words "I'm sorry"—which she wasn't going to—they wouldn't be true.

Next thing Sparrow knew, Mrs. Foxworthy had marched over to the class phone. And the next thing after that, the Solar System kids were back with the teacher's aide, and

Sparrow was following Mrs. Foxworthy out of the room. Walking out, she couldn't see everyone's eyes watching her—but she could feel them. Like being pelted with drops of frozen rain.

Then came the long walk through the halls. Past the orange lockers of the fourth-grade classrooms. Past the big windows that looked out to the empty playground.

When they reached Mrs. K.'s office, the door opened and Mrs. K. sprang out in her teal-colored sneakers, as usual, and a teal romper that reminded Sparrow of Asher's all-in-one outfits. "Head on in, Sparrow. I'll be right there."

Sparrow waited while Mrs. K. and Mrs. Foxworthy talked in the hallway, their voices murmuring. And murmuring. Sparrow wondered what they were saying. Part of her wanted to know. And part of her didn't. It was only going to be about how much trouble she was in.

Finally the voices stopped, and Mrs. K. stepped inside and sat down. "I hear you got in a jam," she said.

She began talking about conflict. How in any conflict there was usually something you might have done differently. She asked what Sparrow could have done instead when Anton began teasing. Sparrow remembered the barking dog coming at her and Toby. *Distance is your friend.*

"Get up and walk away?" she suggested.

"Great idea!" said Mrs. K. They talked about two kinds of distance. Space. And time. Getting up and walking away could give you the distance of physical space. And taking some time to cool down could give you another kind of distance. "I'd like you to wait until some time passes, then think about whether there's anything you might be sorry for. Will you give that a try?"

Sometimes grown-ups asked a question that wasn't really a question. It was an order given in a question-mark voice. But it seemed like Mrs. K. was actually asking Sparrow, not ordering her around.

"Okay," she said, nodding. She already knew she needed to apologize to Anton for stomping on his foot. Not yet, though. She wasn't ready. "I'll think about it."

"Great!" said Mrs. K., clapping her hands together. "Now, looking ahead. You know the Busy Bee poster in your room?"

Sparrow nodded again. "Sure," she said.

On the wall of their classroom was a poster dotted with construction-paper bees—yellow with black stripes—and the numbers 1, 2, 3. These were the classroom expectations.

1. *Be* in your seat. When it's time to work, be in your seat and on task.
2. *Be* focused. Keep your eyes on your work or on the teacher.
3. *Be* a cooperator. Work with your classmates and the teacher.

"Great!" said Mrs. K. "Mrs. Foxworthy and I have an idea to help you keep on track with the expectations." She showed Sparrow a sticker sheet of bumblebees and a small piece of construction paper folded in half. There were five boxes on the paper, one for each day of the week. "Every day that you follow the Busy Bee expectations, you'll get a sticker to put in this booklet," said Mrs. K. "And tell you what. I'll put a sticker here in the Monday box to start you off. Sound good?"

Sparrow nodded.

"Great! Now these," she said, holding up three red checker chips, "will be like reminders."

Sparrow would start every day with three chips. If she needed reminding to be a Busy Bee, Mrs. Foxworthy would collect a chip. If she needed three reminders, she would lose all three chips, so no sticker. But as long as Sparrow had even a single chip left at the end of the day, she would get a sticker. And at the end of the week she would take the booklet home to show her parents how many stickers she had earned.

"This should help make things really clear," said Mrs. K., wrapping things up, "for both you and Mrs. Foxworthy. And to make sure we're all on the same page, I'll give your folks a call too."

↗ 18 ↖

At three o'clock the big double doors of Eastbrook Elementary stood wide open.

"Race you!" shouted Sparrow as she darted through the doorway and took off.

"Wait up!" cried Paloma. "Why are you running?"

"To go see Toby!" called Sparrow, her backpack bouncing up and down as she sprinted past the chain-link fence around the playground. "Don't you want to?"

At the end of the school road, she finally stopped to wait. Paloma caught up, and they turned the corner onto Bridge Street. They were both panting, out of breath from running.

"Of course I do," said Paloma, "but *spill*! What happened when you left the room? Where'd you go?"

"I had to go see Mrs. K.," said Sparrow.

"The lady you see for that lunch thing?"

Sparrow nodded. She had told Paloma about friendship group because it was obvious she wasn't always in lunch anymore, and Paloma had agreed it was silly: Sparrow didn't need help making friends!

"So how come you had to go today?" pressed Paloma. "Like, not for lunch?"

"Partly because when we had group projects, and we were supposed to be talking about weather, I was talking about Toby," said Sparrow. "And partly for kicking Anton." She explained all about the poop scooping and the teasing.

"Anton can be really annoying," agreed Paloma. "So are you in trouble?"

Sparrow hesitated. Usually, she told Paloma everything. Except things didn't feel "usually" anymore. On the days when Sparrow got out of friendship group and out to the playground for recess, Paloma was already playing with Anna and Serenity, and Sparrow didn't always want to tag along. Sometimes, instead of joining them, she roamed the playground by herself, pretending she was being guided by Toby.

She knew that being best friends with Paloma didn't mean Paloma couldn't have other friends. But being best friends felt easier at home than at school. At home it was just the two of them. Like when it was the two of them plus the cats. Then the two of them plus Snowberry. And now it was going to be the two of them plus Toby! That's what Sparrow wanted to talk about. Not the stickers.

"Not really," she said, and took off running again. "Come on, let's race!"

19

At home nobody seemed to be around on the Robinson side of the house. Sparrow's dad wasn't there—no surprise—he would be at work until past her bedtime. Her mom must be upstairs with Asher. She and Paloma dropped their backpacks, ran back out and across the porch, and knocked on the green door to Miss Eileen's side of the house.

"Come on in, Sparrow! And you must be Paloma. Sparrow's mom told me you were coming over."

Toby was sitting in the middle of the braided rug.

"Hi, lovebug!" cried Sparrow. She sank down cross-legged beside him and wrapped her arms around him, and he leaned his whole weight against her while his tail half wagged and half thumped on the rug.

"You can pat him too, if you want," said Miss Eileen to

Paloma, who was standing at the edge of the rug. "Do you like dogs?"

"I mostly like cats."

Sparrow looked at Paloma, surprised. First, Paloma didn't love dogs? And second, how could Sparrow not know that? "You don't like dogs?"

"I don't *not* like them," said Paloma, "but I only like them if they're nice." She knelt down on the rug and reached out her arm, and Toby pressed his big, blocky head into her outstretched hand, like he was saying, *I am nice.* Paloma grinned. "He's nice!"

For a little while they sat around, talking about dogs and cats and kittens and birds. About Toby; and Sparrow's almost-a-cat kitten, Gracie; and Paloma's almost-a-cat kitten, Qwerty. And Snowberry, the pigeon. As they talked, Sparrow and Paloma patted Toby. In a little bit he lay down and rolled over onto his back, so Sparrow could rub his belly. Then she lay down beside him.

"You're two bugs in a rug again," said Miss Eileen.

"Two lovebugs," corrected Sparrow.

"Two lovebugs," agreed Miss Eileen, and when Paloma lay down on the other side of Toby, she added, "Now you're snug as three lovebugs in a rug! This looks like Toby's idea of a perfect way to spend the day. Snoozing away the afternoon with you two."

"Sleepover!" suggested Sparrow.

"Slumber party!" added Paloma.

Miss Eileen laughed. "Too bad for Mr. Lazybones, but it's time for his walk." She took down the leash and the blue FUTURE GUIDE DOG vest from a hook where they were hanging.

Sparrow scrambled up from the floor. "Ready, love-bug?"

"Oh, Sparrow, I'm sorry," said Miss Eileen. "Didn't your mom tell you what I said?"

Sparrow shook her head. "I didn't see her."

"Oh dear. I said it was fine for you to bring a friend over to pat Toby inside the house. But when you're outside walking, you need to be a hundred percent focused on Toby. So no friends on the walk. I'll take him out now, and if you want, you can take him again after Paloma goes home."

"Oh!" said Sparrow, feeling the prickling of tears behind her eyes. Quickly she scrunched her face so they wouldn't come out.

"Wait!" said Paloma. "I have an idea."

Five minutes later Sparrow set off down the street, scanning ahead for possible problems. The coast was clear. So was the pale blue, cloudless sky. Sparrow walked down Hartley Street, counting houses as she went.

One . . .

She couldn't believe what a mixed-up day this was. On the one hand, Paloma had come over and they had snuggled with Toby on the braided rug. And then Paloma had volunteered to hang back and play with Gracie so Sparrow could walk Toby! That was the best-friendiest thing your best friend could ever do.

Two . . .

On the other hand, the stickers.

Three . . .

After this walk was over, and after Paloma went home, Sparrow would find out what Mrs. K. had said to her mom. And what if her mom said that Sparrow wasn't being a cooperator?

Four . . .

And what if that meant she couldn't walk Toby anymore? What if her very first all-by-herself walk with Toby was her last one?

Five . . .

They had come to the place where they always turned around—a gray house with wind chimes hanging from the porch, jingling in the soft breeze. She stopped and asked Toby to sit, and he sat. "Good job, lovebug!"

Except . . . if this was their last walk, Sparrow didn't want it to be over so soon. She looked down at the crack between the sidewalk squares. What if she put her foot over the line? What if she went a little farther?

Sparrow stood on the sidewalk, trying to decide. Go farther or go back? The wind chimes were tinkling, and the air smelled like fresh-cut grass. She was taking so long before giving Toby the next command that he turned his head and looked up at her with his deep brown eyes. Eyes that trusted her. *What are we doing?*

The wind chimes rang again, softly, and Sparrow knew the answer.

If anyone found out she had gone too far, then this would definitely, positively, absolutely be the last walk. Which could not happen. Toby was on his way to being a guide dog, and she was definitely, positively, absolutely going to keep helping. Which meant going back.

She gave Toby the command and they turned around. And straight and tall, they headed for home.

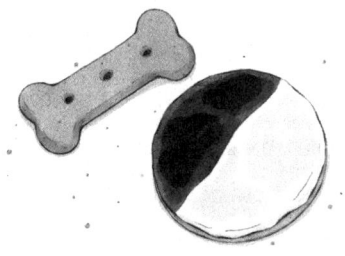

⚹ 20 ⚹

Sparrow sat on the sofa with Gracie on her lap and her mom holding Asher beside her. She was glad they were sitting side by side, instead of facing each other. She didn't like her mom looking right at her. Especially when she knew what was coming next: talking about what had happened at school.

"I heard you had a rough day, Little Bird. Want to tell me about it?"

"Not really," said Sparrow as she stroked Gracie. There was only one thing she wanted to talk about. "But what about Toby?"

"Toby?" asked her mom. "What does he have to do with this?"

"I thought you'd say I couldn't walk him anymore."

"Sparrow, we love that you're getting to walk Toby. That's a great experience for you! Why would we say that?"

Sometimes Sparrow's parents didn't make sense. First they said she could help walk Toby if she was a cooperator in friendship group. Now she was in trouble, so why *wouldn't* they say she couldn't walk him anymore?

"I thought you'd be mad because I got in trouble."

"Sparrow, nobody's mad at you, and you're not in trouble."

This was another thing that made no sense. Mrs. K. might have tried to make the stickers seem like something positive—*follow the rules and get stickers!*—but Sparrow wasn't stupid. The opposite was just as true. If she *didn't* follow the rules, then she *wouldn't* get stickers. And she *would* get in trouble.

And she had a whole list of people who were mad. Mrs. K. Mrs. Foxworthy. Anton. All the other kids in Weather.

She gave Gracie another pat, from the top of her head to the tip of her tail. At least *she* wasn't mad at Sparrow. Unless . . .

Sparrow felt a pinprick of guilt. What if Gracie's feelings were hurt because every day after school Sparrow ran over to walk Toby? What if Gracie felt left out, the same as Sparrow did when she saw Paloma playing with other kids at recess? Quickly she gave the kitten another pat, and Gracie began purring a deep, rumbling purr that made Sparrow feel better. Black splotches on white, or white splotches on black (she still couldn't decide), Gracie wasn't mad at her and never could be. Gracie knew Sparrow loved her.

"I'm not mad," repeated Sparrow's mom, "but you do know you need to apologize to Anton, right?"

"I know!" She wished her mom wouldn't tell her things she already knew. "I'm going to!"

"Good. And you know you're not in trouble, right? Your dad and I are concerned that you're having a difficult time, that's all. So is Mrs. K." Her mom paused and reached over to give Gracie a pat in Sparrow's lap. "So, how's friendship group going?"

Was this a trick question? Mrs. K. had called her mom to tell her what happened today. They probably talked about friendship group too.

"Okay, I guess," said Sparrow. "I still don't get why I have to go, though. Am I supposed to be friends with those kids?"

"You might get to be friends with them," said her mom. "That would be a bonus. But the reason you're there is to learn about some things that are . . . well, not what Mrs. Foxworthy is teaching in the classroom."

"Like what?"

"Like feelings," said her mom. She went on, talking all about feelings. How sometimes it was hard to understand your feelings. And sometimes it was hard to talk about them. Or express them in a safe way.

Sparrow got it. What her mom really meant was that Sparrow's feelings were . . . too much. They made Sparrow get carried away, so she stood on the furniture and

walked away from the teacher and stomped on her friend's foot. And ended up having to do a sticker chart like a baby!

Suddenly Sparrow felt Gracie's paw tap-tap-tapping her cheek. *You stopped patting me.* Sparrow always felt better when she patted Gracie, but right now she felt so stuck that even her fingers felt stuck together. And Sparrow hated that feeling! She hated feeling sticky and she hated feeling stuck. And this was like the worst melted-marshmallow-on-your-fingers, squeezed-in-the-middle-of-the-back-seat-on-a-long-car-ride, sticky-stuck feeling she had ever felt.

"I hate the stickers!" she blurted.

"What's wrong with stickers? We've used them before. We had a star chart for setting the table, remember?"

"Star charts are for babies," said Sparrow bitterly.

"Not necessarily," said her mom. "Dad has a star chart."

"No he doesn't!" cried Sparrow, twisting around so she could look straight at her mom.

"Yes he does," said her mom. She was smiling, but it was a tired smile, and actually, everything about her seemed tired. Her ponytail drooped. Her shirt was saggy, baggy, faded flannel. "It's not a paper chart you can put on the fridge," she explained. "It's an app on his phone."

Sparrow felt like when you did too many cartwheels. Even after you got back to right side up, your brain still felt a little upside down. Why would her let's-get-things-straight, stickler-for-good-grammar dad need a star chart? She kind of couldn't believe her mom. Except her mom wouldn't tell a lie.

"What's it for?"

"You can ask him yourself," said her mom. "Tomorrow morning."

21

Birdsongs came floating through the open kitchen window, like they were catching a ride on the soft May breeze. Through the monitor on the kitchen counter came Asher-waking-up noises.

"Breakfast for you," said Sparrow's mom as she set a plate of cinnamon toast on the table.

"Cinnamon toast, toast, toast," sang Sparrow. "Thank you, thank you, thank you, thank you."

"You're welcome," said her mom with a smile, "and now somebody else will get breakfast upstairs." She disappeared, leaving Sparrow alone with her dad.

Sparrow's mom had cut her toast exactly the way she liked it: crisscross into four triangles. Sparrow picked up a triangle.

She always started with the crust because she liked to save the best part for last. "Dad," she said between nibbles. "Is it true you have a star chart?"

Her dad sat with his hands wrapped around his cup of coffee. "It's true," he said. "Ask me anything."

"What's it for?"

"There's something I try to do every day, so I give myself a star if I do it."

Sparrow nibbled while she listened. Some people would call it meditating, he said. Or praying. He thought of it as taking a moment to sit quietly and be grateful. And the reason he did it was because it helped him be more like he wanted to be for the rest of the day.

Sparrow had nibbled off the crusts of all four triangles. All that was left on her plate were four cinnamony quarter moons. She popped one in her mouth. She loved the way the cinnamon sugar crunched between her teeth and then melted in her mouth.

"Like how?" she asked.

"Like not being critical even when it's my job to correct somebody's mistake. And also—you know—being really nice to you and Mom."

"And Asher," pointed out Sparrow.

"And Asher," he agreed. "Now. Can I ask you some questions?"

"You *can*," she said, "and you *may*."

"Ooh, you got me! Grammar mistake," he said, grinning.

"Okay, my turn. Mom filled me in a little. You want to fill me in some more?"

"It's so unfair!" she began.

Sparrow told her dad how Anton had started the whole thing but she was the one who'd ended up being in trouble. She told him all about the chips and the stickers, and there was a pass card too. That was like a free pass for if there was a time when Sparrow felt she couldn't be a Busy Bee because she needed to step away and get some distance. But it had to be practically an emergency.

Her dad sat with his cup of coffee between his hands. Nodding. Not interrupting. Waiting until she was done to say, "That sounds really hard."

"I thought you were going to say that Mrs. Foxworthy's the teacher, so she's right and I'm wrong."

Now her dad took a sip of coffee. Buying time. The only sounds were the birdcalls breezing through the open window.

"I think Mrs. Foxworthy is trying to be as clear as possible about what she needs from you. So, yes—I think she's right to do that. But that doesn't mean you're wrong to feel that this is difficult. And I get that Anton was . . ." He paused, like he was searching for the right word.

Sparrow was still mad at Anton, and she knew the exact right word. "A total poop!"

A smile flickered beneath her dad's mustache. "I wouldn't say that myself," he said. "But I'll allow it. Now, about those stickers. Mrs. K. wanted me and Mom to talk with you about having a goal and a reward. How about if you get a bumblebee sticker every day for a week, then we do something fun?"

"Do you do that?" she asked. "Give yourself a reward if you get enough stars?"

Her dad shook his head. "My reward is that when I'm doing my thing, I feel better."

She doubted that meeting the Busy Bee expectations was going to make her feel better. But that didn't mean she wouldn't like a reward. She put the last triangle of toast in her mouth. Chewing. Thinking. What would be good? Then an idea came to her, sweet as cinnamon sugar.

22

Family meetings were not Sparrow's favorite. Usually, her parents called them to talk about chores. But this one was to talk about Sparrow's idea, so she was all in. She'd been all in the second she thought of it—which was yesterday—but her dad had said it was time for her to go to school. He would ask Miss Eileen if she could join them for a quick meeting tomorrow morning. Which was today!

Waiting, Sparrow raced around the grass, leaping over dandelions. Half were still sunshine yellow, and half had turned to white puffballs. Finally her mom and dad came outside—her mom holding a cup of coffee, and her dad holding Asher—and Miss Eileen joined them on the porch steps.

"Where's Toby?" asked Sparrow.

"Inside. Practicing waiting."

"Love that concept!" said Sparrow's mom.

"Uh-oh," said Sparrow's dad, jiggling Asher. "Somebody's fussy. Maybe this isn't a good time."

"Let's see if he settles," said her mom.

Sparrow didn't have much time. Soon one of her parents would say it was time for school. "Try swooping him," she suggested. "Uncle Marko said when I was a baby, Uncle Chris would take me outside and swoop me around to make me happy."

"That's true!" said Sparrow's mom. "You always loved make-believe flying."

"And being outside," added her dad, "which is not working for this little guy today."

Asher wasn't all-the-way crying. He was off-and-on crying. Sparrow needed him to be not crying at all.

She darted off the steps and picked one of the white dandelions. Standing in front of her baby brother, she made chipmunk cheeks, then blew the air from her cheeks. Asher's eyes popped wide open as dandelion fluff floated through the sky.

Sparrow did another, and another. Picking dandelions and making them burst apart. A hundred seeds flying off each one like tiny comets in a blue sky. Asher wasn't fussing anymore. In a little while his head sagged and his eyes drooped shut. Sparrow's dad carried him inside.

"That was awesome, Sparrow!" said Miss Eileen.

A minute later her dad came back outside with a cup of coffee and the baby monitor. He gave Sparrow a big smile. "He's asleep. Good job, lovebug."

"All right, let's begin," said Sparrow's mom, "because Sparrow is chomping at the bit."

"Funny thing," said Sparrow's dad, "most people say 'chomping,' but it's actually '*champing* at the bit.'"

"Is chomping wrong?"

"It's not exactly wrong," he said, "but it's technically less correct."

Sparrow's mom made a face that was half amused and half annoyed. She shook her head and raised her eyebrows, giving Sparrow a *Can you believe this guy?* look.

"Dad, I don't think you should get a star today. Mom looks mad!"

Sparrow's parents laughed, and her dad said, "Lucky for me, your mom is a very understanding person. But speaking of stars, yes, let's begin."

He explained to Miss Eileen that Sparrow had a sort of star chart she was working on. And an idea for a reward if she met her goal, her mom added. Then they turned to

Sparrow. They expected her to ask. And to be okay if the answer was no.

"I really want Toby to pass his test," she began, "even though when he goes away, I'm going to miss him. So I was wondering . . . you know how you said he loves to snooze? And we were snug as two bugs in a rug? I was wondering if before he leaves, could we ever have a sleepover? Me and Toby?"

A big blue jay swooped across the sky while Sparrow held her breath, waiting for the answer. Luckily, she didn't have to hold it for long.

"I love that idea!" said Miss Eileen. "And he would love it too. Let's do this."

Sparrow jumped up to grab her backpack. Get a bumblebee sticker every day for a week? No problem!

⭐ 23 ⭐

Half an hour later Mrs. Foxworthy handed Sparrow three red checker chips. That day she didn't take any back, so Sparrow got a bumblebee sticker.

And she had already gotten one yesterday, which was Tuesday. And Mrs. K. had put a sticker in the booklet on Monday, when she was explaining everything, and her parents said that could count. That just left Thursday and Friday. Two days to go.

On Thursday, Sparrow lost one chip, but at the end of the day she still had two left, so she got the sticker. One day to go.

On Friday, Sparrow lost the first chip because of the pencil sharpener. You were only supposed to go sharpen your pencil if nobody else was using the sharpener. Orion was sharpening his pencil, but it looked like he was all done, so Sparrow got up and went over. But then Orion didn't leave. He kept sharpening. And sharpening and sharpening. Sparrow stood and waited, which was not a good use of her time, said Mrs. Foxworthy.

After recess she still had two chips, though, and only a couple of hours to go. She was going to make it! She was so happy, she stopped by Anton's desk as kids were getting settled back in their seats.

"Hey. So you know how I stomped on your foot?"

"You call that a *stomp*?" asked Anton with a grin. "It was more like a *squish*."

"Or a *smush*," said Sparrow, grinning too. "Anyway, I came to say sorry. For real."

"That's okay," he said. "It didn't even hurt."

"Tell that to my mom."

Anton laughed. "My mom says I'm supposed to say sorry too. So, you know. *Sorry.* For real."

They were both laughing when Mrs. Foxworthy appeared and told Sparrow she should have been in her seat by now, and that would be a chip.

And when Sparrow tried to explain, she lost a third one for arguing.

That was week one of the Busy Bee sticker system.

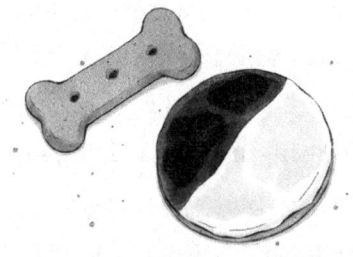

24

Week two of the sticker system began, and Sparrow began noticing something. Orion.

He was over at the pencil sharpener again—the one you had to crank by hand. *Crank-crank-crank-crank-crank.* Then he sat down. A minute later he got up and went over to the electric sharpener. *Whir-whir-whir-whir-whir.* A few minutes later he was back at it—*crank-crank-crank-crank-crank.* Then *whir-whir-whir-whir-whir.* Then over to the pencil jar for a new pencil, probably because he'd sharpened the old one down to a little stub. Back to the sharpener to sharpen the new pencil. Over to the trash to empty out the sharpener, which was probably full of pencil shavings. And spilling them all over the place. Which was when Mrs. Foxworthy went up to Orion and held up a single finger. Which was the same thing she did to signal to Sparrow that she needed to collect a checker chip.

Did Orion have to do the Busy Bee sticker system too? In one way, Sparrow hoped not. She didn't want her and Orion to be the same. He had never said sorry after he accused her of lying about Toby.

In another way, she hoped yes. So she wasn't the only one.

She started paying more attention in friendship group. Sometimes they played games, like Would You Rather? or Apples to Apples. One day all they did was color. Orion's hair had grown so long that his sandy curls hid his face as he bent over his drawing. Finally he sat up. Finished. A winged horse flew over a range of mountains. So many pointy triangle trees ridged the mountains, it looked like there was nowhere for the horse to land.

Isla One gasped. "That's so good!"

"No it's not!" said Orion. He covered the drawing with his hands.

"Yes it is!" argued Isla Two.

"Don't say that!" Orion said, and ripped the paper in half.

Mrs. K. was quiet for a moment. Then she started talking about "I" statements. How if somebody said, "Apples are delicious," somebody else could say, "No they're not." But if somebody said, "I like apples," nobody else could contradict that.

"Let's try to use 'I' statements when we talk to each other," she said. "Orion, I liked your picture very much."

"Okay," he said. "Whatever."

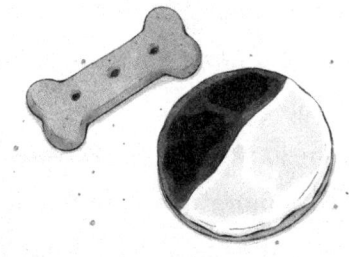

25

Sparrow put the blue FUTURE GUIDE DOG vest on Toby, and they set off. All up and down the street, lilacs made the air smell like flowers. If May were a color, decided Sparrow, it would be purple. There were the lavender-purple lilacs. Purple pansies in window boxes. And purple violets in the grass.

She had asked Miss Eileen if the walk could be longer. Could she go a little farther, maybe for ten houses? Miss Eileen had another idea. She had gone with Sparrow to mark off five houses in the opposite direction. That way the walk could be longer, but Sparrow and Toby could still be spotted from the porch, no matter where they were.

Now Sparrow and Toby walked five houses one way, to the gray house with the wind chimes, then turned around and came back. In front of her house, she passed the spot where the roots of the big maple tree made the sidewalk all lumpy and bumpy. The spot where she had met Toby because she was looking at the sky while she walked, searching for Snowberry.

It was funny. Before Snowberry, Sparrow had never thought much about pigeons. But now she did. Some things were like that. Once you noticed them, it was hard to stop. Like Orion.

I loved your drawing. That's what she could have said to him today. But didn't.

Or maybe she could have said, *I'm supposed to be trying to be a Busy Bee. You too?* She supposed she could still say that. She couldn't imagine talking to him about bumblebee stickers and checker chips, though. Why would he want to? She didn't want to talk about it with anyone. She hadn't even told Paloma!

Sparrow didn't feel great about that. Best friends didn't have secrets. She made up her mind. Paloma was coming over after school again on Friday. She would tell her then.

Back to Snowberry. As Sparrow walked five houses in the new direction, she scanned the sky. She didn't see any pigeons, though. She didn't see any birds anywhere. What she saw were clouds. Huge ones. She tried to remember their name. They looked sort of like the big white ones called cumulus. But these were bigger, and their bottoms were gray. And instead of sailing through the sky, they sat there like they weren't going to budge.

At the fifth house—the farthest she could go in this direction—a voice called, "Hey!"

It was Anton, on his porch. Above his head dangled a flag that changed with the seasons. When Sparrow had moved here last summer, it was bright yellow sunflowers. Then orange pumpkins for fall. Last month it was Easter eggs, and now it was purple lilacs.

Anton bounded off the porch and up to the fence that went around his yard as Sparrow made the *Sit* hand signal. Toby sat, and Sparrow reached into her pocket for a kibble treat. "Good job, lovebug!"

"I can't pet him, right?" asked Anton. He stuck his hands in his pockets, like he needed more than the fence to stop him from reaching out to pat Toby.

"Right," she said, and added, "Thanks."

"You're so lucky," said Anton. "I wish I had a dog."

"He's not *mine*. He's not even Miss Eileen's. She only has him until he takes his test."

Sparrow knew exactly how much longer that was, because yesterday her mom had reminded her that it was less than a month until her birthday, and whom did she want to invite to her party? Paloma and Anton, of course, and how about the kids in friendship group?

Sparrow had told her mom she'd think about it. Friendship group was getting better, but she still didn't think of them as *friends*.

Just then thunder sounded. Not a distant rumble, like

when a storm was far away. A huge, groaning boom, like the sky was mad. *Cumulonimbus!* she remembered—thunderclouds—as Toby made a small whimpering noise.

Sparrow said goodbye, and she and Toby hurried home under a darkening sky. Four houses to go. Three. Two. One. Home! They scrambled up the porch steps to safety as, all at the same time, a zigzag of lightning flashed, a kaboom of thunder sounded, and the rain began.

After a while the thunder and lightning stopped, but not the rain. It was still raining when Sparrow went to bed, and raining when she woke up in the morning.

It kept raining all that next day, and the next night.

The following morning Sparrow woke up. Listened. *Pitter-patter-pitter-patter-pitter-patter-pitter-patter.* It felt like it had been raining forever, making the days blur together.

"Morning!" Sparrow's dad stuck his head through the doorway. "Time to get moving. I'll give you a ride." He held up his hand before she could say she liked walking in the rain. "It's Friday, remember? You have to bring in your poster."

The rainy, blurry day came into focus.

Friday. The day the Weather group was making its presentation.

But also, *Friday!* Paloma was coming over after school.

Finally, Friday. The day she brought home her booklet to show her parents how many stickers she had gotten.

And this week she was on a roll! A couple of days she had lost a chip, but she had never lost all three. She had stickers for Monday, Tuesday, Wednesday, and Thursday.

All she had to do was get through today, and she'd have a perfect week.

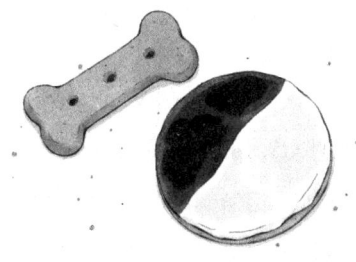

⭐ 26 ⭐

The problem wasn't Weather, exactly. The problem started right after.

Sparrow and the other Weather kids had gone to the front of the room to make their presentation. Sparrow had her cloud poster. Caleb had a poster about wind, and Yasmeen had made a poster about rain that was mostly covered with a rainbow. Harriet was dressed all in yellow and carried a huge yellow construction-paper sun. For stormy weather, Anton had filled a jar with food coloring and dish soap. He swirled the jar around to make the ingredients look like a tornado.

Each of them said something about their type of weather, and Harriet wrapped it up. "Weather is all around us, all the time."

"Thank you!" said Mrs. Foxworthy. "Everyone, let's give

this group some silent applause." She held her hands in the air and wiggled her fingers, and the rest of the fourth-grade class did the same.

"All right," she went on. "We'll have presentations on the Water Cycle and the Solar System next week. Now I'd like all my rising fifth graders—that means everyone—to take out your math workbooks. I don't think I need to remind you that we only have about a month of school left. So let's get busy!"

Get busy?

Sparrow might have been okay if she hadn't still been standing beside Yasmeen, who gave a little gasp. Or if she hadn't heard Harriet and Caleb begin to giggle. Or—fatal mistake—if she hadn't glanced over at Anton, who made a funny face, his mouth and eyes open wide in make-believe shock. Sparrow began to crack up laughing too.

The whole Weather group was in danger of losing it. But Yasmeen's hand flew to her mouth, and Caleb bit his lip, and Harriet managed to ask if she could go get a drink of water, then scooted from the room. They pulled it together.

Anton wasn't pulling it together. He gave Sparrow a wild-eyed, won't-stop-can't-stop grin and kept laughing. Not laughing *at* her, like last time. Laughing *with* her. Because she was nonstop laughing too.

"Anton," said Mrs. Foxworthy. "Sparrow. Can you two settle down, please?"

Sparrow tried to stop but couldn't. She glanced at Anton

and started cracking up all over again. There was nothing to do but get away from him. Get some distance! Without asking for permission or saying where she was going, she ran from the room.

Big mistake.

⤺ 27 ⤻

The rain had finally stopped and the clouds were scurrying across the sky as Sparrow walked home with Paloma. She didn't feel good about having kept a secret from Paloma. It felt good to tell her everything now.

She explained how that day she kicked Anton, Mrs. K. had made her start a whole sticker chart thing. How she got stickers if she met the classroom expectations. And how if she got a sticker every day for a week, she was going to have a sleepover with Toby! But this week was ruined! Because first she had left the room without permission, and then she had refused to explain why.

"Then remember when you and me were talking about you coming over? That was the third time I got in trouble, so I didn't get the sticker today."

"But I didn't get in trouble!"

"You were in your seat," explained Sparrow. "I wasn't."

"That's not fair," Paloma said, then demanded, "How come you never told me?"

There were a million reasons why. Partly Sparrow was embarrassed. Partly she wished it would just . . . *stop*, and she wouldn't have to think about it any longer. And partly it was because she didn't want everyone else to know. And Paloma had so many other friends.

"You're always with Anna and Serenity at recess. And I don't want everyone else to know."

"I wouldn't have told," protested Paloma. "But I get it. But how come . . ." She stopped in the middle of saying something.

"How come what?" pressed Sparrow as they reached the end of the school road and turned the corner onto Bridge Street. In the strip of grass along the sidewalk, yellow dandelions were popping open like little suns in a green sky.

"How come you hardly ever want to play at recess anymore?"

Sparrow didn't have a good answer. It wasn't like Paloma had left her out. She had kind of been leaving herself out. Because she didn't want to share Paloma. At least not with Anna (who wore her hair in a French braid) and Serenity (who wore red beads in her locs)—two kids who both probably knew, just like Paloma somehow knew, that nobody in fifth grade wore kitty-cat headbands.

"There's too many kids. I like it better just us. Sorry."

"Me too," said Paloma.

"You don't need to be sorry," said Sparrow. "You didn't do anything."

"No, I meant I like it just us too."

There didn't seem to be anything to say after that. In a little bit they crossed Bridge Street, then walked past Sparrow's church, a big white building with a steeple. At the bakery they stopped to look through the window. Outside hung boxes of purple pansies. On the other side sat trays of cookies.

"There's your favorite," said Paloma, pointing to the biggest cookies, frosted half vanilla and half chocolate. The black-and-white.

"There's yours," said Sparrow, pointing to the chocolate chunk.

They were standing with their faces pressed so close to the window that their breath was fogging up the glass.

"Don't you think the stickers are ridiculous?" asked Sparrow.

"Totally," agreed Paloma, drawing a smiley face in the fogged-up window.

"I think Mrs. Foxworthy hates me!"

"Yeah, but no she doesn't!" said Paloma, drawing another smiley face. "She took Marmalade!"

That's what Sparrow's mom had said. How when Sparrow was finding homes for their neighbor Mrs. LaRose's cats, her teacher had taken one. So in a way

Mrs. Foxworthy had helped Sparrow help the cats. It was kind of funny when you thought about it. Sometimes you *got* help so that you could *give* help to somebody—or something—else. Either way, giving help and getting help always went together. Like black-and-white cookies.

Sparrow stood staring through another smiley face at the cookies. She just wished she weren't the one who everyone thought needed help this time.

⚔ 28 ⚔

Everything felt washed and clean as Sparrow and Paloma walked the rest of the way home, counting purple things. Shaggy lilacs still dotted with raindrops that glittered in the sun. Tulips as big as coffee cups. The lilac flag at Anton's house. Mrs. Baxter's purple house with its matching purple bird feeder, which was across the street from Sparrow's house—where something seriously strange was going on.

Out in the front yard stood Miss Eileen with Toby, Sparrow's mom with Asher in a sling, and her dad—how come he was still here?—all wearing T-shirts and shorts, and tall rubber rain boots. And scattered on the lawn was all their stuff. Well, not *all* their stuff. But tons of stuff. Laundry baskets full of wet laundry. Soggy cardboard boxes. Rakes and shovels. Gracie's carrier for going to the vet. All the stuff that was usually in the basement.

"What's *up*?" cried Sparrow. "What's happening?"

"The basement's flooded," said her dad.

"Like, *underwater*?"

"You can go look," said her mom. "But stay on the stairs! Do not go all the way down! Got it?"

"Got it!" cried Sparrow as she and Paloma raced into the house and halfway down the basement stairs. At the bottom, water covered the floor. Not deep, like a swimming pool. But everywhere, like a giant puddle.

Back outside the grown-ups were still talking about water, which seemed a little more interesting now that there was a giant puddle in the basement.

"I still don't understand how this could happen," said Sparrow's mom, running her hand up and down along the big bump that was Asher in his sling.

"Rain?" suggested her dad. "It's been raining for days, and off and on before that all spring."

"I know that! But Mrs. LaRose never said anything about the basement flooding."

"It happens, though," said Miss Eileen, Toby sitting at her side. He wasn't wearing his blue vest, and instead of sitting up straight and tall, he was leaning against Miss Eileen's legs as she scratched the top of his head. "You can have a dry basement for years, and then one year the ground will be so saturated, the water has nowhere else to go."

"So now what?" asked Sparrow's mom.

"Now I go to the hardware store for a water vacuum," said her dad.

"And we can talk about next steps," said Miss Eileen. "If you want."

Sparrow's parents both gave a *yes, please* nod, and Miss Eileen went on.

"You can try digging a trench all around the house and filling it with gravel, which should help. If that doesn't work, and the basement keeps flooding, you can put in a pump that pumps water back outside. Water coming in and out isn't ideal, of course, but it's not the worst thing."

"What's the worst thing?" asked Sparrow.

"Stagnant water," said Miss Eileen. "Water that simply sits there, not moving. That's when you get problems like mold and mildew and bad smells." She gave Sparrow a smile and scrunch-wrinkled her nose to make a bad-smell face, then turned back to Sparrow's parents. "But we won't let that happen. Best-case scenario, we can stop water from coming in again. Next-best work-around: we'll make sure any water coming *inside* gets moved back *outside*."

"Thank you so much," said Sparrow's mom, "for everything. For helping us move all these things outside, and for being an expert on water!"

"Looks like we picked the right tenant," said Sparrow's dad.

"Like Sparrow wanted!" piped up Paloma.

"Yeah," added Sparrow. "Like I told you to!"

Everyone laughed, and there was a bright, sun-coming-out-after-the-rain feeling. Overhead, red cardinals flitted from tree to tree, and in the grass, honeybees buzzed from dandelion to dandelion, guzzling nectar. Then Sparrow's dad turned to her.

"Hey, how'd we do today? Is it a five-bumblebee week?"

Sparrow shook her head.

"Sorry, honey," said her mom in a sympathetic voice. "Better luck next week."

"We know you're trying," added her dad. "Mrs. Foxworthy says most days are going well."

Sparrow wasn't surprised that her teacher was in touch with her parents. She *was* surprised that Mrs. Foxworthy thought she was trying. She *was*. But something always seemed to happen.

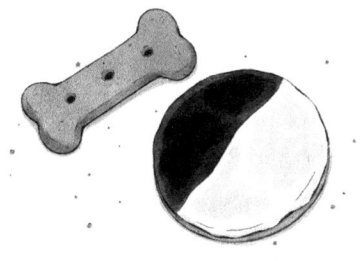

29

Sparrow's turn.

Holding her breath, she reached toward the tower and drew out a block, and the Jenga tower stayed standing. She let her breath go. Time to read aloud the word printed on the block.

"'Surprised,'" she said.

There were three ways they could communicate the feeling word that was printed on their block. One: make a face. Two: describe what the feeling felt like in their body. Or three: tell a story about a time when they'd had that feeling.

Sparrow almost always chose the making-a-face way because the other two ways needed words, which was harder. She opened her mouth and her eyes as wide as they could go, like Asher's face when he saw the dandelion fluff floating in the sky.

"Well done!" said Mrs. K. with a big smile. The teal highlights dotting her hair looked extra bright today. They made Sparrow think of robin eggs in a nest. That wouldn't be a very peaceful nest, though. Along with being a smiler, Mrs. K. was a big head-nodder. She was always smiling and nodding at you when you talked.

"Your turn, Isla."

Isla One slid out a block and read the word printed on it. "'Brave,'" she said. "When I go to the dentist, I'm supposed to be brave."

"'Supposed to be' isn't a feeling," objected Isla Two.

Isla One made a mouth-in-a-straight-line annoyed face.

"We aren't criticizing anyone else's responses," reminded Mrs. K. "Your turn, Isla."

Isla Two pulled out a block and read the word. "'Guilty.' That's like when you sneak cookies and eat a whole bunch and get a stomachache."

"Wait," said Isla One. "Are you doing the story or the feeling in your body?"

Isla Two took one of her two pigtails in her hand and twirled it around her finger. Thinking. "Both!" she said. "I did swipe a bunch of cookies once and eat them. That's the story. And I did get a stomachache. That's the feeling."

"A twofer!" cried Mrs. K., making a thumbs-up. "Two for one. Well done, Isla."

"Did you throw up?" asked Orion. "After you ate too many cookies?" He was swinging his legs, as usual. Mostly his feet just bumped the legs of his chair, but sometimes they almost grazed the legs of the table. Sparrow wished he would stop. He'd knock over the Jenga tower if he wasn't careful.

"No," answered Isla Two, but Isla One said, "I did! One time we had lobsters and then blueberry pie and I had a stomachache and then we were playing freeze tag and then I threw up."

Sparrow was wondering if Mrs. K. was getting mad that the feelings Jenga game was getting off track, but Mrs. K. didn't look mad. She was still smiling and nodding. "Do you remember how you felt after you were sick, Isla?"

"Good," said Isla One. "Better."

"There are some feelings that we don't mind having. Like feeling peaceful. Or thankful. And there are other feelings—kind of like stomachaches—that we often wish we weren't having. Like guilt. Or sadness. Or anger. But it doesn't help to simply wish that a feeling would go away, or to pretend we're not experiencing that feeling. Any ideas for what we can do?"

Miss Eileen's face popped into Sparrow's head. The wrinkle-scrunching face she'd made to show the bad smells you'd get if the worst thing happened. Water in a giant puddle. Not moving.

Sparrow chimed in, "Move them from *inside* to *outside*?"

"Yes!" Mrs. K. made a quick fist pump with her hand. "Any ideas for how to move feelings from inside"—she laid her hands on her teal dress, then held them out in the air—"to outside?"

"Say them out loud?" suggested Isla One.

"Write them down?" suggested Isla Two.

"Drawing?" suggested Orion.

Mrs. K. was giving a *yes* fist pump for every idea, but Sparrow thought it wasn't that easy. Maybe some kids could put their feelings into words or pictures, but not her.

It was Orion's turn. He reached toward the tower, and Sparrow held her breath—it felt like everyone was holding their breath, hoping the tower wouldn't topple—as he pulled out a block. The tower stood.

"What's the word?" asked Isla One.

Orion was staring down at the block. Not reading the word aloud.

"What is it?" pressed Isla Two.

Orion still wasn't answering. He was swinging his foot

again. Back and forth. Sparrow sneaked a look at the block he held in his hand, and in the second before Orion's foot knocked the table leg and the Jenga tower came crashing down, she read the word printed on the block.

LONELY.

30

Outside it was the usual. Shouts ringing in the bright blue sky. Kids on the blacktop, playing four square. Kids on the climbing wall, scrambling as high as they could go. Kids on the grass, running to the far edges of the playground, up to the chain-link fence.

Everyone was on the move except Sparrow. She was standing by the playground doors, waiting for Orion. Wondering what Mrs. K. was saying to him. She had told Sparrow and the two Islas it was time for recess, and asked Orion to hang back for a minute.

"Hey!" called Paloma, running up to her. "Me and Anna and Serenity are gonna play popcorn four square. Come on!"

"I can't," she said. "I'm waiting for Orion. Mrs. K. kept him back after lunch."

"Plaid-shirt Orion is in your lunch thing?"

This reminded Sparrow of the kitty-cat headbands—Paloma noticing what other kids did, or didn't, wear.

"Yeah, but he had to stay late. And so what if he always wears plaid shirts? Who cares?"

"I'm just kidding," said Paloma. "Anyway, I heard there's a rule they can't take away your recess."

It was weird to think about grown-ups following rules. It seemed like all they did was make rules for kids to follow. And if Mrs. K. couldn't *make* Orion stay in for recess, what was happening?

"So, what's up?" pressed Paloma.

"I have to ask him something," Sparrow began, and then stopped. She didn't think she should tell Paloma the whole story. How Orion had knocked over the Jenga tower when he pulled out the "lonely" block. How he had torn up his drawing of the flying horse. How she thought he might be doing the Busy Bee sticker system too, and she wanted to find out.

"Well, come find us," said Paloma. "If you want to play."

Sparrow hesitated. "Orion too?"

"Sure," said Paloma with a shrug. "But he might be mad at me and Anna. He doesn't like what we're doing in the group project."

"What are you doing?"

"You'll see!" said Paloma as she ran off.

Sparrow wasn't even sure what she would say to Orion if she did talk to him. Maybe just that he wasn't the only one who was supposed to be getting bumblebee stickers. She was too. So she knew how it felt.

But she never got a chance to tell him because he never showed up at recess that day. He didn't come out the next few days either.

And she couldn't talk to him during lunch in the cafeteria because there were way too many other kids around. Or at the next friendship group lunch because Isla One and Isla Two were there.

And she couldn't risk talking to him in Mrs. Foxworthy's room because that was sure to cause a checker chip situation. Sparrow had already messed up the last two weeks, and there were only a couple of weeks left until her birthday. Until Toby went away.

Which meant she could. Not. Lose. Any. Chips.

⚡ 31 ⚡

So far so good.

So far Sparrow had gotten a sticker every day this week. Monday. Tuesday. Wednesday. On Thursday she got her fourth sticker—only one more to go!—then hurried home to walk Gracie and Toby.

"Your turn first today," she said as she put Gracie's red harness and leash on the kitten. Outside, Gracie padded a few feet across the grass, then stopped and sat and began licking her paws and washing her face.

All around, it felt like spring was going wild. Birds were cutting across the sky. Whirlybirds were twirling down from the maple tree. White fluff was still drifting off the dandelions, leaving the bare stems standing there like they had lost their hats.

Standing and waiting, Sparrow decided that walking a

cat was the exact opposite of walking a dog. It didn't feel like either she or the kitten was standing up straight and tall, ready to do a good job.

Except that wasn't fair. Gracie didn't have a job the way Toby was going to have a job, helping somebody who couldn't see. Her only job was to be adorable. And when Toby left to do his job, Gracie would still be here, being adorable.

Right now being adorable meant Gracie still wasn't walking anywhere, so Sparrow plunked down on the grass beside the kitten, and they began the game Sparrow called back-and-forth. Sparrow held out her hand, and the kitten walked along beneath it, from the crown of her head to the

tip of her tail. Her fur was warm from the sun. When the end of her tail had slid through Sparrow's hand, Gracie turned around and went back the other way.

Back and forth the kitten kept going. Back and forth on the green grass, under the blue sky. Back and forth under Sparrow's outstretched hand.

"All right, Graciebug," Sparrow finally said, "good job being adorable."

Time to walk Toby. Sparrow put Gracie back inside and brought Toby out. They walked five houses in one direction, toward the house with the wind chimes. Then turned around and walked back to the lumpy, bumpy sidewalk in front of Sparrow's house. Then set off the other way, toward Anton's house. They were almost there when she heard a dog barking.

"Toby, sit," said Sparrow. Toby sat and looked up at her—*Aren't I great?*—and Sparrow looked around.

Problem. It was the same barking dog that Miss Eileen had crossed the street to avoid. On their side of the street. Coming toward them.

Now what?

Sparrow felt hot and cold at the same time. Like when you swallowed something too spicy and your whole head felt hot. But frozen cold too. Like she couldn't move.

Bark, bark, bark.

Now what, now what, now what?

32

"So then what?" asked Paloma.

"So I didn't know what to do!" said Sparrow. "If I tried going home, we'd go right past the dog!"

She had started off telling Paloma, but a bunch of other kids had gathered around too. Anton, of course. Yasmeen and Harriet. Anna and Serenity. Henry and Owen and Ahmed. And Orion, standing by his open locker like he was looking for something inside. But Sparrow was pretty sure he was listening.

"And I didn't think we should cross the street, because the rule is be on the sidewalk where Miss Eileen can see me. And I couldn't keep going 'cause that's too far—"

"She can't go farther than my house," chimed in Anton, rocking back and forth on his feet.

Sparrow could tell he was trying hard not to blurt out the whole story. "Plus, the dog would still be right behind us," she added.

She had remembered how Miss Eileen said sometimes a dog had to disobey a command to keep the person safe. Was this like that, but opposite? Was *Sparrow* supposed to break the five-houses-this-side-of-the-street rule to keep *Toby* safe? Except she had felt like she couldn't move. Like even her brain was so frozen that she couldn't decide!

First bell rang—the one that meant announcements would start soon. Kids from other classes streamed down the hallway to their rooms, and half the kids who were bunched around Sparrow took off, heading into Mrs. Foxworthy's room.

"So then what?" pressed Paloma.

"She saw *me*!" burst in Anton, a big smile on his face.

Sparrow didn't even care that Anton had finished her story. When she had seen him on his porch, standing under the lilac flag and waving, it had felt like her brain had unfrozen. With Toby trotting at her side, she scurried to the safety of his fenced yard. She wasn't on the sidewalk where Miss Eileen could easily spot her. But she had put some distance between Toby and the barking dog.

"So me and Toby went to Anton's," she said, wrapping up the story right as second bell rang—the one that meant announcements would start *really* soon. There was the *slam, slam, slam* of lockers closing, and almost everyone else peeled off and hurried into the classroom. The only kids left were Anton, Paloma, and Orion.

Suddenly the voice of Principal Weiss came over the loudspeaker—"*Good morning, Eastbrook Elementary*"— and Anton bolted for the classroom, followed by Paloma, who called over her shoulder, "Hey, let's play guide dogs at recess!"

That left only Sparrow and Orion in the hallway.

She lifted her hand and gave a little wave. "Hey."

"Hey," he echoed. Today his plaid shirt was big blue and green stripes crisscrossed with white. "That's so cool you get to walk that dog. Sorry I said it wasn't true."

"*Hot lunch today is veggie pockets.*"

"That's okay," she said, and asked, "So where were you at recess this week?"

"*Happy birthday to Isabelle Brunsman.*"

"Mrs. K. lets me stay in her room and draw if I want."

"*Fourth graders, please let your teacher know if you want to welcome your classmates to school on next year's morning announcements!*"

Sparrow was about to ask Orion if he was doing the Busy Bee sticker system too, when Mrs. Foxworthy appeared in the doorway. "Seats, please!"

Sparrow knew she could make it to her seat before the end of announcements if Mrs. Foxworthy would just give her a second.

"Be right there," she said.

For a moment nobody moved. Everybody stood still. Sparrow and Orion in the hallway. Mrs. Foxworthy in the doorway. Then Sparrow's teacher held up a single finger—*one*—and disappeared into the classroom.

One chip. That's what the finger meant. Sparrow had lost a checker chip. That wasn't good, but it wasn't horrible. One chip lost meant she would still get a sticker, and that would make five stickers for the week. Which meant: Toby sleepover.

"Did you see that?" asked Sparrow, holding up her pointer finger like Mrs. Foxworthy had.

"Yeah. Guess I lost a chip."

"Me too," she said, and suddenly they were both smiling.

"And now from all of us to all of you, welcome!" said Principal Weiss. Which was when Mrs. Foxworthy appeared in the doorway again, holding up two fingers.

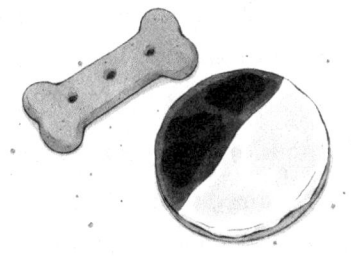

33

Two checker chips gone. One left.

Sparrow trooped outside with Mrs. Foxworthy's class, wondering if it was possible to get through the rest of the day without losing a third chip. Of course it was *possible*. But also, something always seemed to happen. Except it couldn't. Not for the rest of the day. Not if she wanted to have a sleepover with Toby.

"All kids who are *not* in the Solar System group, please pick a spot," called Mrs. Foxworthy.

Sparrow scrambled onto one of the big stone blocks arranged in a semicircle that made up the outdoor classroom, and Anton sat down beside her. The air was warm—finally it was T-shirts, shorts, and sandals weather—and the sky was blue, streaked with long trails of clouds. Sparrow knew their name now: cirrus.

"I see everyone sitting," said Mrs. Foxworthy when all the Weather kids and the Water Cycle kids had found a seat, "and now I want to hear everyone listening."

She stepped back and stood beside Mrs. K., in her teal romper, and motioned for Henry, one of the Solar System kids, to step forward. Hang on—what was Mrs. K. doing here?

"The solar system," announced Henry. Through purple-framed glasses, he began reading from a piece of paper. "The solar system is all the planets and other things in space that go around our sun."

As he read, kids ran to take their places.

Right beside him stood Serenity. The sun.

Ahmed ran a few feet out to be Mercury.

Next came Owen, a few more feet away. Venus.

Anna was Earth, and Paloma was Earth's moon, circling around her.

Henry kept calling out names. The group of Solar System kids waiting their turn got smaller and smaller. The distance they ran got farther and farther away. Mars. Jupiter. Saturn. Uranus. Neptune. Finally there was only one kid waiting his turn. Orion.

"And the last planet," said Henry, "is Pluto!"

As Henry explained that Pluto used to be called a planet but was now considered a dwarf planet, Orion trudged across the playground. It seemed like he was walking forever. How far did he have to go to be in the right spot? wondered Sparrow. He was halfway across the playground, almost to the monkey bars!

Finally he stopped. Even though he was so far away, she could see how he stood with his head down and his hands in his pockets, kicking the dirt with his sneaker. Rocking back and forth.

Anton nudged her. "What's up with Pluto?"

"Paloma said he didn't like what they were doing," said Sparrow. "Maybe he feels left out."

"He's not left out," objected Anton. "He's still in the solar system."

"But he's the farthest away."

Sometimes—lots of times, really—Sparrow felt like her feelings were stuck inside her, making her feel stuck too. She knew she wasn't good at getting her feelings out. But she was pretty good at telling what feelings other people had. Usually it was right there on their faces. Mrs. Foxworthy's disappointed-in-you face. Asher's surprised face. Sparrow's mom's face when Sparrow's dad corrected her: half annoyed and half amused.

Sparrow couldn't see Orion's face from here but she could see his whole self. Kicking the dirt and rocking back and forth like a Jenga tower about to topple.

Her mind began darting all over the place.

Friendship group. The last block pulled from the tower: "lonely."

The walk and the barking dog. Seeing Anton on his porch and suddenly knowing where to go to feel safe. Toward a friend.

She could tell Orion needed a friend.

But the chips. The stickers. *Toby.*

↗ 34 ↖

"Be in your seat." That was the rule.

Sparrow remembered Mrs. K.'s work-around for choosing between two things: mocha chip ice cream. There was no work-around for this, though. Nothing in the middle. Sparrow could follow the rule or break the rule.

Except there was no way Sparrow could stay in her seat. No way she could follow the rule. She couldn't think about the rules or the Busy Bee sticker system. And she definitely couldn't think about Toby, because if she thought about Toby, she might not go. And she had to go. Because if somebody needed help, you had to help.

After clambering down from the big stone block, she streaked past Mrs. K. and

Mrs. Foxworthy. She flew past Henry, who had stopped reading his solar system report. Past Serenity and Ahmed and Owen and Anna. Past Paloma and the other kids.

Halfway across the playground, she pulled up. She had run so fast, she was out of breath.

"What's up?" asked Orion. He had stopped kicking the dirt. "Why are you here?"

"I just, um . . ." She paused, panting. "Came to say hi."

"That's kind of random," he said with a puzzled look on his face. Like he wasn't sure about her. If she was really his friend or not.

Sparrow was still panting. Still trying to catch her breath. Trying to think of something to say so he'd know she was there for real, as a friend. She grinned when she thought of it. "And I wanted to ask—want to come to my birthday party?"

"Okay!" he said, a big grin appearing on his face too, like the last piece of a puzzle slipping into place.

In the distance Sparrow spotted people on the move. The Solar System kids were heading off the playground, back toward the big stone blocks of the outdoor classroom.

Mrs. K. and Mrs. Foxworthy were going in the opposite direction, trotting out to where Sparrow and Orion stood.

In a moment they were there. Mrs. K., with her teal streaks in her hair, and Mrs. Foxworthy, with her red glasses perched on her head. Sparrow figured her teacher was going to hold out her hand—the signal that meant she needed to collect a chip. But Mrs. K. spoke first.

"Is everything okay, Sparrow?"

Sparrow nodded. "Yeah. I had to . . . ," she started, then stopped. She had come out here because she thought Orion was lonely. But how could she say that out loud? She didn't want to embarrass Orion.

"Take your time," said Mrs. K. She put her hand on Sparrow's shoulder. "Would you say there was an emergency?"

She gave a *yes* nod of her teal-spotted head. "Something you needed to use the pass card for?"

The pass card! Sparrow had forgotten all about the pass card. It came back to her now, from the day Mrs. K. had explained the system. If she ever had to do something that *wasn't* meeting the expectations—"Be in your seat," "Be on task," "Be a cooperator"—she could use the pass card. But it had to be an emergency.

"Yes!" blurted Orion. "It was an emergency. She had to invite me to her birthday party."

Mrs. K. and Mrs. Foxworthy looked from Sparrow to Orion to Sparrow. Then they began looking at each other the way her parents did sometimes: *What do you think? Well, what do you think?* Then they were smiling at each other.

"Well," said Mrs. K. finally. "That *is* very important. Don't you agree, Mrs. Foxworthy?"

Mrs. Foxworthy nodded. "I do," she said. "I do agree."

✧ 35 ✧

A soft May breeze drifted through Sparrow's open bedroom window. Sparrow was in her bedroom, but not in her bed. She was on the floor, with Toby. And Gracie. And Paloma, and Paloma's kitten, Qwerty. One, two, three, four five. Snug as five bugs in a rug. All asleep, except Sparrow.

She lay awake, remembering.

What Mrs. K. and Mrs. Foxworthy had said. That they could call it a very good use of the pass card.

What Miss Eileen had said: "Sounds like a good example of intelligent disobedience."

What her dad had said; "I wish I could have seen you, streaking like a comet across the solar system!"

What her mom had said: "You're a great kid, Sparrow."

Through the open window came the sound of a car

driving down the street. Down the hall came the sound of Asher crying—just for a little bit, until her mom or dad must have picked him up. And right beside Sparrow came the sound of Toby as he made a soft, contented sighing noise in his sleep.

36

Sparrow was supposed to be cleaning her room. It was Sunday afternoon, and the sleepover was over. Toby was back on his side of the house. Paloma and Qwerty had gone home. It was just her and Gracie.

Sparrow picked up a dirty sock from the floor and tossed it for Gracie to chase. The sock sailed across the room and slid under the bed, but Gracie didn't race after it. She began washing her paws, as if she were too grown-up and dignified to chase socks anymore. Sparrow went and knelt down to reach under the bed. Felt something funny—not a sock—and pulled it out.

Her kitty-cat headband. The one she used to wear every day. The one she thought was lost.

She slipped on the headband. It had been so long since she'd worn it that it felt a little funny. Not funny like it hurt.

More like funny . . . different. She went into the bathroom and stood on tiptoes so she could see herself in the mirror. Same cinnamon freckles. Same light brown hair in two braids. And back again—cat ears!

But did she look babyish? And what did that even mean, anyway?

"What do you think, Gracie?" she asked. "Kitty-cat headband, yes or no?"

Gracie was winding figure eights around Sparrow's bare ankles. It didn't matter to her. She loved Sparrow without the kitty-cat headband. She loved her with it.

The next school day, the halls of Eastbrook Elementary were thronged with kids, as usual. Sparrow zigged and zagged through the crowd, on the lookout for headbands. She spotted one kid with a rabbit-ears headband, two kids with unicorn horns, and a single third grader with cat ears. The headband craze was definitely over.

When she reached the lockers outside Mrs. Foxworthy's room, Paloma was already there.

"Your headband!" she cried.

"Yeah, I found it," said Sparrow.

"It looks cute!"

"Thanks," said Sparrow, wondering, what if she had called Paloma to say she was wearing her headband today? Would Paloma have worn hers, too, if Sparrow had asked?

Because something felt different, like the way the headband felt a little funny now. It was easy to be best friends at home, when Paloma came over. Home was kittens and Snowberry and Toby. School was different. School was where Paloma cared about whether something was cute or not cute, which Sparrow didn't really care about.

"Hey," said Paloma, "did you put your name in to do the welcome tape? Today's the last day! Wouldn't that be cool if we both got picked? Then next year, even if we're not in the same class, you'll hear me and I'll hear you!"

"Yeah, but is that fair? All I know is *oui, bonjour, bienvenue, c'est la vie.*" Sparrow ticked off the words she knew. "'Yes,' 'hello,' 'welcome,' 'that's life.'"

"So *ask* if it's okay! Come on: I'll be your best friend!" said Paloma in a coaxing voice, then added, "Oops, I already am!"

That felt good. Maybe she and Paloma didn't care about all the same things anymore. But she still cared about Paloma, and she knew Paloma cared about her.

And when your best friend called "best friend," you said, "Okay."

⤳ 37 ⤳

A wild, it's-almost-summer feeling filled the school. The halls felt extra big because the biggest kids were gone. It was step-up day, and the fifth graders were spending the day at the middle school. And it was the day the new welcome tape was being made.

Morning announcements began. Hot lunch. Birthday wishes. *"Please come check the lost and found before the end of the year to see if anything is yours."* Then: *"Will the following rising fifth graders report to the office?"* Sparrow heard Yasmeen's name and saw her stand up with a big smile on her face. She heard Serenity's name. Names of kids from the other fourth-grade classes. Suddenly Paloma was standing. Then: *"Sparrow Robinson."*

Sparrow grinned. Stood. Filed out of the classroom with the other kids whose names had been called.

In the hallway Paloma stopped at her locker. "Hang on. I have to get something." She tugged on the locker's silver handle to open it and began rummaging around inside. When she emerged, she had a big smile on her face, and on top of her head, her kitty-cat headband. "Surprise!"

Kitty-cat headbands perched on their heads, just like before, Sparrow and Paloma strode down the hallway. Sparrow had that straight-and-tall feeling, like Toby when he wore his blue vest. Like she was going to do something important.

She also had the feeling that this might be the last time she and Paloma would wear the headbands together, but that was okay. Fourth grade was almost over. Next year they were going to be the new big kids.

In the office, waiting her turn to use the microphone, she still had the straight-and-tall feeling. She couldn't decide if she wanted to say *bonjour*, which meant "hello," or *bienvenue*, which meant "welcome." She was still trying to decide when she glanced through the big glass window between the office and the front-door lobby and spotted her parents walking into the school.

What are they doing here? she wondered as her parents spotted her, too. They smiled at her through the window, waved, and kept on walking down the hall. Where were they going?

And how come, when Sparrow and Paloma got back to

their classroom, the teacher's aide was in charge and Mrs. Foxworthy was gone?

Sparrow ran through the same questions all over again at lunch.

"Maybe you're in trouble for kicking me," said Anton. "Maybe they were going to see the principal."

"No," said Paloma. She had nabbed the table where they were sitting—one where fifth graders usually sat. It was like she was calling it for next year. "That's old news."

"Besides," said Yasmeen, "the principal's office is right next to the front office. If they didn't come in there, they must have been going somewhere else."

"Yeah, but where?" asked Paloma. "And how come Mrs. Foxworthy was gone?"

Sparrow opened a waxed paper bag and pulled out a slice of green apple. Green apples were her favorite. Sweet, but tart, too.

"They were going down the hall," she said, suddenly picturing where that hallway led. "Maybe they were going to talk to Mrs. K.!"

Munching an apple slice, she remembered how her mom had said she was such a great kid. She remembered the big smiles on the faces of Mrs. K. and Mrs. Foxworthy out on the playground with Orion. Maybe instead of being in trouble, it was just the opposite.

"Maybe I'm going to get an award!"

"For *what*?" cried Anton. "For never being in your seat?"

"For being *nice*," said Paloma.

"Yeah," chimed in Yasmeen. "For being nice."

"Yeah, for being nice," echoed Sparrow as she popped another slice of sweet-tart apple into her mouth. She liked the sound of that. An award.

⊀ 38 ⊁

Walking home, Sparrow felt like she was floating. Like she was striding down the hall with Paloma, kitty-cat headbands perched on their heads like crowns. Rising fifth graders. Best friends.

Her house came into view. White house. Green doors. And her mom in a pink sundress, sitting on the porch steps. Waiting.

"Hey, Little Bird," said her mom, "sit with me." Her hair was pulled back with a scrunchie, like usual, but it was a saggy, tired-looking ponytail. She handed Sparrow a glass of lemonade.

Sparrow shrugged off her backpack, sat down, and guzzle-gulped half the lemonade.

"So," began her mom, "you're probably wondering why Dad and I were in school today. We had a meeting with

Mrs. K. and Mrs. Foxworthy. First, Mrs. K. said she was so proud of you for being a good friend to Orion."

Sparrow nodded. She already knew that, but it felt good to hear it again.

"Second, she suggested a pause on the sticker system, and Mrs. Foxworthy agreed. They feel you understand the expectations."

"I do!" cried Sparrow.

She tilted back her head and chugged down the last of her lemonade, making her mouth feel sweet-and-sour zingy. Her whole insides felt zingy now.

"I got picked to do the tape!" she announced.

"That's awesome!" said her mom.

"I couldn't decide whether to say *bonjour* for 'hello' or *bienvenue* for 'welcome,' so I said, '*Bonjour* and *bienvenue*!' and the secretary said it was okay!"

"Sounds like Sparrow being Sparrow," said her mom, smiling.

Sparrow leaned against her mom, and her mom draped her arm over Sparrow's shoulder and gave her a squeeze. Sparrow nestled into the sideways hug for a minute, then scrambled up and announced, "I'm gonna go do Toby's walk."

"Hang on," said Sparrow's mom. "There's a couple more things."

Sparrow sat back down on the porch step.

Everyone agreed that Sparrow was trying, said her mom, and that she had been a super cooperator in friendship

group. But she and Sparrow's dad had still requested that the school do some special testing.

"What kind of test?" asked Sparrow, thinking about Toby's test. How if he didn't pass, he wouldn't get to be a guide dog. "Like the kind if you don't pass, you stay back a year?"

"No!" said her mom. "It's not that kind of test, about how much you know. It's to figure out how you learn best. So you'll be set up for success in fifth grade."

Sparrow still didn't like the sound of that. It sounded like something a teacher would say. "When?" she demanded.

"Not right away," said her mom. "Sometime before the end of the school year, though. Probably in a couple of weeks."

Sparrow's head was buzzing. *Bonjour, bienvenue.* Fourth grade, fifth grade. Friendship group, and the things they had done there. Two truths and a lie. Drawing. Feelings Jenga: surprised, brave, lonely. The test. And Toby's test, which was coming up soon and which—if he did well—meant she might never see him again.

"You okay, Little Bird?" asked her mom, draping her arm over Sparrow's shoulder again and trying to draw her close. "You want a hug?"

"No thanks." Sparrow hadn't minded a happy hug, but the last thing she wanted was a hug that was supposed to make her feel better. What she wanted was to be with Toby. "Can I go walk Toby *now*?"

"Of course," said her mom. "There's one more thing, but we can talk when you come back. It's about your birthday."

↗ 39 ↖

May had turned into June, which Sparrow decided should be white, if it were a color. Or maybe pink. Or both! Up and down Hartley Street, crab apple trees were losing their petals. Tiny pink petals and tiny white petals sailed in a warm, blue-sky breeze, along with giant bubbles that kids were making from a big tub of soapy liquid on Sparrow's front lawn.

It wasn't Sparrow's actual birthday, but it was her birthday party. She was having her party today because on the day of her real birthday her whole family was going to go along with Miss Eileen to watch Toby take his test. That was going to be her present.

But right now Miss Eileen in her blue polka-dot shirt and Toby in his blue vest were here, watching but staying out of the way of the kids running around. Paloma, obviously.

Anton, along with the other kids from the Weather group: Caleb and Harriet and Yasmeen. Plus the kids from friendship group. Isla One, Isla Two, and Orion.

Suddenly a screen door creaked open and banged shut, and Sparrow heard the first words of the song.

"Happy birthday to you."

Then her mom was coming down the porch steps carrying a cake, while her dad carried Asher.

"Happy birthday to you."

Her mom put down the cake on the folding table that had been set up in the yard. "Happy birthday, dear Sparrow."

It was decorated like a giant black-and-white cookie!

"Happy birthday to you."

"Make a wish!" cried Anton.

The candles were burning down on the black-and-white cookie cake, and everyone was waiting. Old friends: Paloma and Anton. New friends: Yasmeen and Orion. Her mom and her dad and Asher. Her uncle Chris with his freckled face just like Sparrow's and her mom's, and Uncle Marko with his curlicue mustache. Miss Eileen and honey-colored Toby with his deep brown eyes, standing straight and tall in his blue FUTURE GUIDE DOG vest.

For a tiny second Sparrow thought about Toby. She imagined her and him and Gracie lounging around on the floor of her room. Or sitting at the kitchen table with Gracie in her lap and Toby at her side. But she had already

made up her mind about that, and she wasn't going to change it back. She couldn't wish for Toby to be her dog. Miss Eileen had spent a year teaching him to be a good dog, so he was ready for the test, and Sparrow had even helped a little. She couldn't wish for him to fail.

What about *her* test, though? For another second she thought about using her candle-blowing wish on that. For the test to show that she didn't need any extra help.

Because she still didn't much like the idea of *getting* help. She'd rather be a help *giver*. She'd rather be the kid who found homes for Mrs. LaRose's cats, and who rescued Snowberry from the storm and got her to a bird sanctuary, and who took Toby on walks. The kid who raced across the playground to stand with Orion. All those things had felt, well . . . *good*.

Except maybe the whole help thing wasn't like the two sides of a black-and-white cookie. Maybe it was all mixed up, like Gracie's black-and-white splotches. You weren't only a helper or only somebody who got help. You could be both. She could be both.

Sparrow decided. Getting out of getting extra help was not how she was going to use her nine-going-on-ten birthday wish. She drew a deep breath and blew out the candles.

"What'd you wish for?" asked Orion.

"She can't say!" said Paloma.

Sparrow couldn't say her wish now, but she could say it later. On her real birthday, when she turned ten. After her wish came true. For Toby to pass his test. So he could have harness training with a real trainer. So someday his vest would just say GUIDE DOG. So he could be a helper, and somebody could get the help they needed.

"Tell you later," promised Sparrow.

*I*t was finally here. The day of my test. The people who would decide if I was good enough for harness training stood off to the side in the big room. One of them was making a video. They weren't the only people there, though. Hiding behind a big piano and some plants in pots, watching, was Miss Eileen, of course. Plus Mr. and Mrs. Sparrow and the baby. And standing on tiptoes so she could see—Sparrow.

The tester walked me up and down a little ramp. He walked me between some chairs squished close together. He walked me by a plant that some other dog had peed on to see if I would try to stop and pee too. No way! That's against the rules.

Miss Eileen had told Sparrow that the test would take only about ten minutes. I don't really know what that means. All I knew was that everything was going so fast. Somebody brought another dog into the room. Somebody made a loud sound. I ignored all that.

The tester was making another round of the room. We went by the piano. I didn't look at Sparrow, but I knew *what she was thinking:* You got this, Toby! *And not to brag, but I knew I did. I was nailing it!*

Suddenly it was over. Miss Eileen was allowed to come out and say hello, along with Sparrow and her family. We hadn't heard the official result yet, but I think we all knew. I had done it!

Sparrow was making a funny face, with a crumpled, trying-not-to-cry smile. Like she was half happy and half sad. I knew the feeling. Half of me was super excited that I was on my way to being a real guide dog. Half of me was super sad to say goodbye. Sad for me, because I was going to miss Sparrow. And sad for Sparrow. It was good to know that she would still have Gracie.

Then Sparrow's smile totally crumpled. Tears started falling from her brown eyes and rolling down her cinnamon-freckled cheeks. I wanted to lick the tears off her face, but I knew that wasn't going to fly, so I just wagged my tail as hard as I could.

I was trying to tell her: *I'll always remember you, Sparrow. And I hope you'll always be the Sparrow I knew. The Sparrow who gets carried away because she cares about things so much. So don't worry about whatever that test ends up saying. Whatever you find out, remember: you don't need to change. You're going to grow up, but you don't need to grow out of anything. You'll grow into all the things that make you you. You'll grow into yourself, Sparrow.*

And in my book, that's awesome. You got this, Sparrowbug.

Acknowledgments

I am grateful to the helpers. To Lee-Anne Leverone from Guiding Eyes for the Blind for sharing her knowledge of raising puppies to be guide dogs. To Catherine Hewitt and Katie Campbell for sharing their elementary school insights. To the fellow writers who guided Sparrow's story to fruition: Ann Harleman, Charlotte Agell, Debra Spark, Elizabeth Searle, and Maria Padian. To Elysia Case for capturing Sparrow in her beautiful images, and to everyone at Atheneum who made the Sparrow books better through their caring, careful work—Erica Stahler, Kaitlyn San Miguel, Karyn Lee, Kristie Choi, Olivia Ritchie, Sophia Jimenez, and Tatyana Rosalia. I appreciate you all.

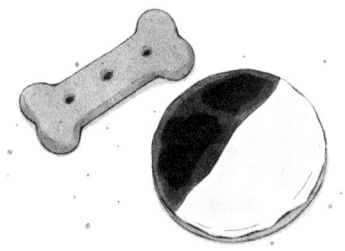

A Note to Readers

We all have different ways of learning. Sometimes school feels like it has one way of teaching and something is wrong if you don't learn that way. Kids might feel funny if they get pulled out of class for extra help. They might worry if grown-ups say they need testing—which doesn't sound fun. It's okay to have these feelings and to be nervous about being different. It's good to know that testing can be a way to get tools that help you learn—like getting your eyes checked for glasses when you can't see the board in class, or getting fitted for new sneakers when your feet grow. Knowing more about yourself and how you learn makes it easier to feel like you belong and still be your own authentic self.